Love Will

Cindy Brunk

Disclaimer

Love Will is a work of fiction. Names, characters, businesses, places, events and incidents are either the products of the author's imagination or used in a fictitious manner. Any resemblance to actual persons, living or dead, or actual events is purely coincidental.

Published in Hood River, OR 2015

First Printing July, 2015

ISBN: 1494457776
ISBN-13:9781494457778

DEDICATION

To my first child - **Adam**

Who was with me for such a short time, yet will

always have a piece of my heart.

.

CONTENTS

Acknowledgements

To my husband- John

Hey love, thanks for putting up with me as a writer. Come to think of it, for all the other times as well! I love you.

To my children- Ruby, Rose, Sara, and David

The honor of being called Mom by you is the highest accolade I have or ever will achieve. Thanks for all your wonderfulness and support.

To my Editor- Emily Keith

Your editing skills are astounding. You have a great future ahead of you and I hope to have the opportunity to repeat the experience. I truly could not have done it without you. Thank you.

To my Mom - Diana Barnes

Many of the experiences gathered while serving in the ministry took place with your support. Thank you.

To my dear friends- Deborah Tilden and Kris Mooney

Your encouragement and prodding were instrumental. Thank you.

To my Cover Designer- Rose Brunk

You have a unique eye for design. I can't wait to see where it takes you! Thank you.

To my Cover Photographer- Amancay Blank Photography

Your skill at capturing emotion through photos is astounding. Thank you.

To my Co-Writers- You know who you are

This journey was far from solo. I'm honored that you trusted me with the intimate details of your lives, and I pray that you will find comfort and a sense of accomplishment in the end result. Thank y

Preface

LOVE WILL was born out of a desire to give hope to those hurting from the choice of abortion and to educate others about the trauma that many may be experiencing yet be unable to pinpoint.

My personal experience with post-abortion trauma, as well as many years serving in the ministry, have resulted in a deep awareness of the devastation one may face after the procedure.

LOVE WILL carries a message. Because the spiritual wounds from abortion can run so deep, it's important that the issue be approached gently. The more the pro-life movement's message transitions from judgment towards compassion, the more effective it will be.

The majority of the book came to me in my mind like a movie. The biggest challenge was finding words to adequately express the emotions. The entire process took nearly two years, though it was set aside often for weeks.

It is my hope that the messages in this book will bring about civil discussions regarding abortion and its aftermath.

If you're facing an unexpected pregnancy or are hurting after an abortion, please see the letter and resources listed at the back of this book. Please know there are many who desire to help.

1. A MORNING FAR FROM TYPICAL

Jordan

This was not a typical Friday morning for high school senior Jordan Parrish. Jolting from bed two hours early seemed far from ideal, but his outlook improved when a delicious familiar smell wafted into the room. He'd have just enough time to wolf down two homemade buckwheat waffles before heading to school for the homecoming court coronation practice.

It was an honor to be voted onto the court by his classmates, especially since he'd been the new kid just last year. He really missed his family, the farm, and the small town that would always be home, but the move to the city had been a sacrifice worth making.

Liz, Jordan's mom-away-from-home, tinkered with her many ongoing projects while Jordan ate. "Your folks are on their way. See you at the game. Have fun and be smart," she called out as Jordan, his mouth still full of waffles, slipped on his letterman's jacket, grabbed his fully stuffed backpack, and headed for the door.

It was an exciting time in his life, with the homecoming football game tonight, the dance tomorrow, and the team's district championship in a week. He loved football but couldn't wait for the season to end, since it signaled the beginning of his favorite season. Wrestling was his real passion, and the 11 years he'd invested had paid off, landing him three full-ride college scholarship offers.

Jordan, remembering how much he loved this woman, walked over, gave her a big hug, and replied in a deep voice, "You always say that. Thanks for being here, Liz, It means a lot.

Paul

Paul, dreading his back-to-back counseling appointments scheduled for the day, took the first bite of a homemade blueberry muffin. The fast pace of the busy mental health organization melted away while he examined the triple frame photo collage displayed on the desk in the large corner office.

His eyes were drawn to his wife's thick black hair, long enough to blow across both their backs as they stood overlooking the rugged waters of the Pacific Ocean. He remembered not having a care in the world on that first of many trips to Mexico. The discomforts that came along with camping on the rocky beach paled in comparison to the beauty of the sunsets, the excitement of snorkeling adventures, and the satisfaction of gorging on inexpensive lobster dinners.

He noticed Heather's hair was still long in the next photo, though not quite as thick. The face of the caramel-colored puppy cuddled in her arms was barely visible as they stood beaming with excitement in front of their first home, a tiny cottage in a neighborhood full of young families.

In the third photo, her shoulder-length hair surrounded a face displaying both joy and heartache. She and Paul were lounging near the pool in the nicely landscaped backyard of a much larger home, five children clamoring for the highly-valued center position on Aunt Heather's lap.

In an attempt to avert another looming migraine, Paul took a long deep breath, pulled out his cell phone, and pressed the first speed-dial option.

"Hello?"

"Hi, hon. How was your appointment? And please tell me you're on hands free," he said, attempting to sound nonchalant.

"It was fantastic, and of course I am," she chuckled. "Baby's great. Had another ultrasound and saw her sucking her thumb. Can't wait to show you the still shot. Doc says things couldn't be better."

Letting out an audible sigh of relief, Paul settled in to enjoy chatting with the woman he'd adored for more than 20 years. The outlook for his day no longer seemed so daunting. He could sense Heather's excitement as she continued. "I *even* found an adorable Easter dress at the mall. With little yellow and green polka dots..."

Wendy

Wendy's grip tightened around the steering wheel of her shiny black Audi. It was bad enough that the presentation for her biggest client had kept her up until just before 3 a.m. but now she was going to be late as well.

"I am sick and tired of rescuing you! If you'd just lay off the drugs, you'd get your license back and wouldn't have to rely on the school bus. We *all* have to deal with alarms and deadlines. Keep this up, and you won't need to worry about college because *you won't even be accepted,*" she shouted with disdain while glancing repeatedly towards the passenger seat.

She saw her little sister sink deeper into the heated leather seat, pulling the hood of her tattered jacket tight around her face. Wendy's agitation grew as it became apparent that Meg was once again checking out. Like so many times before, she was torn between trying to help her and giving up completely.

Leaning forward to determine if it was worth continuing, Wendy expected to see Meg zoned out or even sleeping. What she did *not* expect to see, however, was the dark blue color of Meg's lips and fingernails and the erratic jerking motions of her arms. Wendy gasped as she noticed the stop sign flashing past just outside Meg's window. Her arms felt like cement as she threw one across Meg's face and the other across her own.

Heather

The glare of the late morning sun and the heavy traffic had little effect on Heather's mood. There were too many good things to think about instead. Their baby was healthy, her business was growing, and she was chatting with her best friend. Maybe she'd take him to the mall tomorrow to see the nursery furniture that had caught her eye.

A flash of black appeared less than a second before Heather heard the sound of shattering glass. Everything went into slow motion as the left side of the car seemed to take on a liquid form, caving in around her. She was barely able to place both arms around her belly before the seat belt tightened and the airbag inflated, leaving her tightly pinned down.

Paul

Paul recoiled from the phone at the sound of the collision. Then, realizing it was his *only* connection to Heather, he jammed it back against his ear.

"Heather? Please tell me you're okay," he begged.

The only thing he could hear over the still-connected hands-free system was the muted sound of moaning and coughing.

Paul had no idea where he was going, but remaining at his desk was simply not an option. He knocked over the coffee cup, dousing the last bit of muffin as he grabbed his keys and wallet and bolted for the door.

No one in passing dared ask Paul questions as he exited the building. It was obvious from his expression that interruptions would not be welcomed. With the phone still pressed tightly against his ear, he kept his eyes riveted on the slowly descending floor numbers in the elevator. *God, I know we haven't talked much, but please help my wife and child*, he pleaded.

As Paul moved out of the elevator and into the parking garage, he listened intently, attempting to discern the muffled words, possibly *smoke* and *fire*.

All of a sudden, he heard a voice that sounded as if the person were standing right next to him.

"Ma'am, I'm sorry I have to be so rough," he heard, followed seconds later by the sound of an explosion, then total silence.

Paul slumped to the cold cement floor as he felt the explosion leap through the phone and travel straight to his heart. Unable to focus on any one of the many thoughts swirling around in his head, he did his best to remain calm.

Am I all alone now? Is she feeling pain? Is she even alive? Is our baby alive? This can't be happening. Where was the accident? Am I dreaming? Who did that voice belong to?

The sound of sirens speeding past snapped him back to reality, allowing a transition to the logical mode of operation that suited him so well.

There was no way of knowing exactly where the accident happened, but he *did* know that Heather had been to the doctor that morning. There were two hospitals in the area. One was close to the doctor's office, but the other had a large shopping mall nearby.

She'd been hesitant to buy anything for the baby, but the doctor was optimistic this time. She must have gone to the mall after her appointment, he told himself.

Paul snapped into automatic pilot and rose from the floor. Finding his car was easy, unlike the traffic he had to battle on the way to the hospital.

Liz

Liz was deep in thought while ripping out the last of the plants from her garden. She did her best to brush the dirt off her hands before answering the phone stashed deep in her pocket.

"Hello, this is Sergeant Devon Walker, I'm hoping to reach Liz Modrich, guardian of Jordan Parrish," she heard.

"This is she, " Liz replied hesitantly. Though there was *never* a welcome emergency call, none had ever come with a tone this somber.

"Ms. Modrich, I need to inform you that Jordan's been seriously injured while assisting at the scene of an accident. He's currently being life-flighted to Mercy Medical and I suggest that family and loved ones get there as soon as possible."

"Thank you," was all she could say.

Liz was grateful that Jordan's parents were just now arriving on the far side of the city, although that circumstance didn't make passing along the news any easier. She knew her husband Charles would be home within minutes of hearing the news. At times like this, she couldn't get into his comforting arms quickly enough.

2. TRIAGE

Paul

Paul didn't even notice the couple he stepped in front of as he approached the emergency room admitting desk.

"Wife was in traffic accident- is she here?" he blurted to the woman behind the desk.

"There've been several injury auto accidents so far today, and I'll be able to assist you right after I help the people who entered before you," she stated in a professional manner.

Embarrassed, Paul nodded in agreement. "I'm sorry," he said to the couple, granting them access by stepping aside.

"How can I help you?" asked the clerk.

"We've been told our son is being life-flighted here. His name is Jordan Parrish," answered the man.

Paul listened as the clerk informed the couple that the chopper carrying their son had just arrived, but it would be some time before they could see him. She gave them a clipboard with several forms attached and let them know that a nurse would come out to the lobby to collect it and bring them up to speed on their son's condition.

When the couple stepped away from the desk, Paul quickly filled their spot, desperate to know if he was in the right place.

"What is your wife's name, please?" the clerk inquired.

"Heather Saunter, is she here?"

"One moment please," the clerk replied while searching the hospital database. "She's on her way via ambulance. It's taking longer than usual due to traffic. They should be arriving soon."

"How badly is she injured? Is the baby alright?" Paul asked.

"I'm sorry, but at this point the only information I can give you is that she's on her way," the clerk stated while handing him a clipboard. "Here's some forms to get started on. You'll see the ambulance when it pulls up."

Despite the cloud of apprehension filling the lobby, the couple that arrived before Paul remained upbeat. Paul leaned ever so slightly in their direction in order to eavesdrop. He had to find something to occupy his mind since the clock on the wall was driving him mad with its agonizingly slow rate.

"You know," the man said, "it's hard to believe that 18 years have passed since he was born. It seems like just yesterday. Man, I couldn't wait to get my hands on him."

"Yeah, I remember when I got the first glimpse of his black hair, it was so different than all the others," the woman added. "And when he started nursing, it felt like a dream."

Moments later, a nurse with fiery red hair sporting a hint of grey came barreling through the double doors from the ER to the lobby. Her pace slowed when she noticed the couple she needed to speak with was praying.

"Mr. and Mrs. Parrish?" she inquired.

"Yes," he replied. "My name's Trevor and this is my wife Karina."

"My name's Rhonda, I'm Jordan's nurse. He's unconscious and has sustained serious injuries, the most concerning being head trauma. He wasn't involved in the initial accident but was injured while rescuing a pregnant woman trapped in her car."

As she reached out to touch Karina's shoulder, Rhonda continued. "He got them out just before it exploded, even shielding them when it did. His head was injured when it was hit by debris. Your son's pretty amazing."

"Thank you. We've known that since before he was born," Karina agreed with a nod.

"I'll be back to get you as soon as the doctor gives approval, and just so you know," she continued softly, "I'm praying for him, too."

Just then, two ambulances pulled up to the Emergency Room entrance. Rhonda was right behind Paul as they went out to greet them.

Stepping aside to let the first group pass by, Paul noticed the young lady on the stretcher appeared conscious yet oblivious to her surroundings.

"Meg," implored the professionally dressed woman keeping time with the fast-moving entourage. "Meg, please, I love you. We can get through this. Stay with me," she pleaded.

The back doors of the second ambulance opened slowly, and the EMTs were moving in a calm and low-key manner. Following their cue, Paul took a long, deep breath, slowed his pace, and waited while they carefully removed the patient.

He could see Heather's forced smile through the clear oxygen mask. Her eyes were full of tears and both hands clutched her belly.

Paul bent over and kissed her forehead, whispering, "I love you." He then lifted her hands, moved his face down to where they'd been, and whispered, "I love you, too."

He grabbed one of Heather's hands and with questioning eyes looked at the EMT in charge.

"Yes, you can stay with us," the young man responded to the pleading look in Paul's eyes, "but we *do* need to get moving".

Karina

Back in the lobby, a phone rang from the bottom of Karina's purse. Jordan's school counselor was concerned by his absence at the coronation practice.

"No, he won't be at the game tonight." Karina stammered as the fear began to creep in. "He's in the ER, and actually he won't be returning to school for... Gosh, I don't know... if ever."

After passing the phone to Trevor, Karina returned to her purse. Digging out the small Bible and turning quickly to

Isaiah 43:2, she meditated on the scripture that never failed to bring her peace.

> *When you pass through the waters,*
> *I will be with you;*
> *and when you pass through the rivers,*
> *they will not sweep over you.*
> *When you walk through the fire,*
> *you will not be burned;*
> *the flames will not set you ablaze.*

Hours passed before Rhonda once again appeared, motioning for Karina and Trevor to join her. "He's still unconscious and will be moved to ICU soon. The doctor wanted to bring you up to speed before then," she shared while ushering them through the double doors.

The volume of activity in the emergency room was high and Karina couldn't help but overhear snippets of information while passing through the long corridor of areas sectioned off only by fabric dividers.

She heard quiet sobbing in one, followed by the sound of a child's resistance to treatment in the next. As two staff members sped by, Karina overhead, "…sister found the empty pill bottle in her purse, we're intubating now, may be too late."

She could hear a doctor filling in the impatient man from the lobby. "The tape is showing some mild contractions," he said.

"It's happened before. I can't tell her again," the man muttered.

This must be the woman Jordan rescued, Karina thought as they hurried past. Finally Rhonda stopped and motioned them into a room with real walls and a closing door.

At first Karina was relieved to have the privacy but quickly realized she would've preferred that it not be necessary. She grabbed Trevor's hand as they entered what appeared to be a scene in a primetime medical drama.

Was Jordan really the one in there? Instead of a bed, Karina saw a robotic-looking device suspending a body facedown on a well-padded sling. The head was bandaged and cradled in a way that appeared to be holding it together. Pushing the Humpty Dumpty nursery rhyme out of her mind, Karina continued taking it in.

The entire backside of the patient was covered in loose, wet bandages, and tubes entered the body in numerous places. Her senses were overwhelmed by the sounds of humming machines, beeping monitors, and the smell of sterility.

Karina noted the contrast of this environment to the sights, sounds, and smells of the cow barns she had been in just that morning. The image of Jordan, barely four years old, wearing rubber boots and carrying a big stick as he gently guided the cows into the barn flashed through her mind.

Returning to her current reality, Karina saw that several staff were attending to the patient, but only the doctor made eye contact with her and Trevor. He then wisely stepped aside, giving them a chance to comprehend the scene.

Realizing that anything the doctor said would be irrelevant until her mind accepted that it truly was him, Karina lowered herself to the floor enabling her to scrutinize what could be seen of the bandaged, swollen face.

She searched for the often-questioning, deep, brownish-green eyes, but they were closed. Next she looked for the shiny thick black hair, but it was completely covered, or *was it even there anymore*?

Finally her eyes settled on the tattoo of a cross on the uncovered right shoulder, which triggered the memory of a recent conversation. Jordan's dimples had been in full glory as he convinced her of the significance of the tattoo he'd be getting, now that he was 18 and no longer needed her permission. She was ready to listen now.

Dr. Pennington started in, "Your son has third-degree burns over nearly half his body *and* is unconscious due to head trauma. We've started him on morphine and we're prepping him now for a CAT scan to determine the damage and to look for possible bleeding in the brain. We'll be taking him from Radiology to the operating room, where we'll place a probe in his skull to monitor any swelling. The severity of the burns alone makes his prognosis quite serious, but we'll know more after the CAT scan. Do either of you have any questions before we move him?"

Trevor looked at Karina, who shook her head, then replied, "No questions, but can we have a quick moment alone with him?"

"Of course, we can give you about three minutes." he agreed while motioning for the staff to step out of the room.

Kneeling together and pressing in, the couple was intent on getting as close as possible to their son in spite of all the cold hard metal between them. They'd been in this situation with Jordan before, with very little probability of his survival. Like before, the list of reasons things would not go well was much longer than the list of reasons they would. And once again, they reached out to the only source they could place their hope and trust in.

"Heavenly Father...".

Rhonda

Rhonda was passing by Jordan's room just as Dr. Pennington exited.

"I've given them three minutes," he said.

"Transport's on its way," she responded without missing a beat.

Rhonda overhead Wendy on the phone as she continued down the hall.

"Mom, I've got Meg at the ER. She's overdosed again. Please call back!"

Paul stepped away from Heather's bedside as Rhonda approached and introduced herself. Although giving heartbreaking news was nearly an everyday requirement of her job, this kind always seemed to be the most difficult.

"Though you might not even feel them, the monitor is showing some contractions, which of course we must do our best to stop," she said to Heather. "You're receiving Cyanokit through the IV to counter the effects of smoke inhalation, and we've increased your dosage of progesterone. Once we get you to your room, your bed will be inverted to take pressure off your cervix. Your OB doctor as well as Jorie, our counselor on staff, will be stopping by today." Rhonda reached out and gently touched Heather's arm as she continued. "I know nothing I say can make things better, but please know that I understand what you two are going through. Do you have any questions for me in the meantime?"

"No, but thank you," Heather managed to whisper before turning her head away, allowing the tears to flow.

"By the way, "Paul interjected with reproach as Rhonda passed by, "No one understands unless they've been there."

With a sincere and gentle smile, Rhonda replied, "I absolutely agree, and I *have* been there- *five* times. I'll be back shortly to help move Heather to her room."

She brushed away the single tear slipping down her cheek as she continued her rounds. Rhonda had been loving on people long enough to realize she shouldn't take Paul's comment personally. It was obvious he was hurting.

A quick stop at the drinking fountain provided the only respite Rhonda could afford. She splashed water on her face, and took a long drink, with memories of losing her little ones playing like a slideshow in her mind. She was grateful for her two children and the new grandbabies in her life, but her arms still ached for those she'd lost and what could have been. She said a quick prayer for Paul and Heather, then reminded herself it was time to get back to work.

Rhonda was adjusting several dials, reducing the flow of medicine keeping Meg sedated, when Wendy returned to her sister's curtained-off chamber.

"Hi, Wendy. My name's Rhonda, I'm the nurse assigned to your sister."

"Nice to meet you, Rhonda, and thanks for helping her."

"It's my pleasure. Will your parents be here soon?"

"I called both of them. Dad should be here any minute, and I left a message for mom," replied Wendy as she lowered herself into one of the chairs in the corner. Her hair, which had been pulled back tightly in a chignon, now cascaded over a crestfallen face and drooping shoulders.

Rhonda, sensing that Wendy was struggling, sat down next to her.

"What's on your mind?" she asked.

"I feel horrible about what happened," Wendy admitted. "I was really upset, yelling at her, not watching the road. It's been torture seeing her throw everything away. She had so much going for her, it's bad enough *she's* so messed up, but now *others* have been hurt as well."

"Wendy, do you think your sister looks up to you?"

"Yes. Well she *used* to anyway, but I don't think she looks up to anyone now. Why do you ask?"

"Well, *I'm* willing to bet she still does, and I'm hoping you'll do the same. You could have a huge impact on how willing she is to accept the help she needs. Because Meg's 18, your parents can't *force* her into rehab. And besides, it's more effective if she does it willingly."

"I'll do whatever it takes, *if* I even get the chance," Wendy promised, looking over at Meg and witnessing the first signs of movement.

"Chances are good that you will," added Rhonda as she too noticed Meg's movement. "I'll ask Jorie, one of our staff counselors, to stop by. She's a great resource and can give you advice about talking with Meg. Right now I need to let the doctor know she's waking."

Meg

Despite Meg's determined will to keep them going, the beautiful, multicolored, swirling lights filling her mind were rapidly fading into the distance. She could hear a familiar voice becoming louder and more distinct. "Meg, please wake up. I'm so sorry. Meg, please. Things will get better," her sister pleaded.

The comforting lights were but a memory now, and there seemed to be no stopping the unwelcome flood of reality.

Meg's reluctant eyelids slowly opened. Through the fogginess, she could barely differentiate the faces before her: Wendy and a stranger stood closest to her, with Mom and Dad in the background.

"What the hell is this?" she shouted indignantly, realizing the restraints on her hands made it impossible to extract the tube impaling her nose.

The bright lights sent jolts of searing pain through her eyes and into her head, only to be met by the reverberations of what seemed like every possible sound in the world.

Meg, preferring her previous state of consciousness, closed her eyes tightly with hopes of returning to it. Finding only blackness in place of the beautiful lights, and not wanting to talk with anyone, left her no other option but turning her face away.

Shit, I thought for sure I took enough this time, now they're all gonna be asking questions. Why can't this just be over, she thought to herself.

"I don't want to be here," she muttered out loud.

"Why don't you want to be here, Meg?" asked the soft-spoken stranger, standing near her bed.

Still facing the wall, too tired to hold back and angry that this stranger knew her name, Meg retorted loudly,

"Because I'm just fucking tired of it all, and I want it to be over."

"Meg, my name's Jorie, I'm a counselor here at the hospital. Do you know how you got here?"

"Of course I do," Meg sneered, still facing the wall. "Screwed it up as usual. Skipping school, took a bunch of pills, then Wendy called. I saw it was her- shouldn't have answered. *She* must have brought me here."

"No Meg, your sister picked you up to take you to school. She was distracted when she saw how sick you were, she ran a stop sign and hit another car. You arrived here by ambulance."

Opening her eyes as she turned her head, Meg glared straight at Wendy and, seething with accusation, declared, "So I guess I can't blame you *this time*."

Wendy took a deep breath, then responded with soft, carefully-chosen words. "Meg, this is not just about you and me. There was a pregnant woman in the other car. She was rescued by one of your classmates just before the explosion. She might lose the baby, and your classmate's in critical condition."

"People lose babies all the time," Meg stated callously. "Who's the classmate?"

"His name's Jordan Parrish; do you know him?"

Meg's hostility evaporated as she closed her eyes, turned her head away and whispered "Yes". It was obvious to all that she was finished with the conversation.

Wendy

Jorie nodded at Wendy as she stepped back from the bedside.

Wendy pulled a chair next to the bed and sat down, placing her hand next to Meg's, being careful not to touch it. She was grateful for the encouragement and advice Jorie had given her and was committed to doing whatever it took to help her sister.

"Meg, I understand you're done talking, and that's okay. I'll respect that. *I'd* like to continue if that's alright with you. I promise I won't demand a reply."

As hard as it was, Wendy waited for a tiny nod from her sister, giving her permission to continue.

"I'm so sorry for *any* part I've had in leading up to where we are right now. I really want to help you, and it's obvious what I've been doing so far isn't working. So I want you to know that I've spent some time with Jorie, and I think she can help us, both of us. You need help withdrawing from the drugs and figuring out why you need them, and I need to learn better ways to communicate my feelings."

"When I didn't know if you were going to wake up, I started to remember all the time we spent together at the beach when we were kids. Do you remember the time we were on the big tree-stump-turned-pirate-ship and how we were dreaming about what we'd be when we grew up? I remember you saying you wanted to have enough children to fill a minivan. Then on the way back to our campsite, we passed that big family that seemed to have at least 10 kids. The two older ones were fighting over who had to entertain the baby while the parents set up camp. You looked over at me and without missing a beat said, 'well, maybe just a Mini Cooper!'"

Wendy's chuckles transitioned to tears, and she realized how exhausted she was. Before laying her head down onto her hand, she sat up tall to sneak a glimpse of Meg's face, still turned away. *Could that be a small smile?* she wondered.

Remembering her promise not to demand a response, she simply waited. There was a lot at stake at that moment, and she realized the importance of keeping her word. Wendy had no idea how many minutes passed before she felt her sister's pinky finger slip softly around hers.

3. SETTLING IN

Jorie

It'd been Jorie's idea to place the large aquarium in the ICU lobby, and clearly the couple sitting next to it were reaping the benefits.

She saw they were holding hands and watching the tropical fish swim in and out of a ceramic castle as she and Dr. Pennington approached later that evening.

"Mr. And Mrs. Parrish, this is Jorie Clayton, our counselor on staff. She'll be assisting you during Jordan's hospitalization." He said. Pausing just long enough for quick handshakes and greetings, he continued, "The CAT scan shows that the damage to Jordan's skull is minimal and should heal without surgery. There was no indication of bleeding in the brain and as of right now the swelling is minor and most likely will be controlled with medication. If things go as I suspect they will, he'll need to be in ICU over the weekend, then will be moved to a regular room."

"When do you think he'll regain consciousness?" asked Trevor.

"That's the wildcard, and we can't make any promises," replied the doctor. "Jordan's in a coma, but due to his age and the good news we've seen on the CAT scan, there's *potential* for a full recovery. However, that potential decreases the longer he's in the coma. There are some environmental factors that can affect his odds, which is why we've brought Ms. Clayton on board. She'll be able to take it from here, and the nurses will keep you updated on any changes in his condition. I'll be touching base with you in the morning."

As Dr. Pennington went on his way, the three remaining adults adjusted their chairs and settled in for a much-needed conversation.

"First of all," the counselor began, "please call me Jorie. I can imagine how overwhelmed and concerned you both must be right now. It's not easy for parents to see their child in such a state of uncertainty. I want you to know as your counselor I can provide consultation regarding the medical questions that come up, help you process your feelings, and support you through this time."

"We'd love to have your help," replied Karina.

Jorie noticed both of them taking a deep breath and releasing some of the tension within. She loved this part of her job. Though she could do little for their son directly, she could have a great impact on his recovery by supporting those closest to him.

"I want to start by providing an explanation of the Glascow Coma Scale and where Jordan's current condition falls on it," she stated while handing them a brochure with the information she'd be summarizing.

"The scale is composed of three tests: eye, verbal, and motor responses. The three grades for each of these tests are scored both separately as well as their sum. The lowest possible GCS or sum is 3, which represents deep coma or death, while the highest is 15, representing a fully awake person. Jordan currently has a score of 5."

Trevor, unimpressed with the numbers, tapped his foot ever so slightly, waiting for news of some action that he could be taking to help his son.

"I know it may appear like there's nothing going on as he's unresponsive," Jorie continued. "However, we know that people have recalled events, such as hearing music, and voices of people visiting them, when they've woken from their coma. I've also read studies about brain scans showing pain interpretation sites lighting up when stimulus is applied to an unconscious person's body. "

"It would be natural for you to feel helpless at this time, but it's important to be optimistic. There are several things you can do to help him recover."

Sensing that the news he needed was coming soon, Trevor sat up tall in his chair and leaned forward.

Karina readied her pen, prepared to take notes as Jorie continued. "Play his favorite music, even if you don't like it. Share with him the things he does that make you laugh or your favorite memories, carry on conversations with others that come to visit him, hold his hand. Apply lotion to his hands and feet, giving him a gentle massage. The bottom line is the more stimulation he receives, the better chance he has of recovering."

"Heather, the woman Jordan rescued, and her husband are providing you with accommodations in a nearby house for the entire time Jordan's here. We're really hoping this makes it possible for one of you to stay and be with him daily."

"We've already decided that Karina's staying," replied Trevor, relieved to have a plan of action taking shape. "Having the room for her is such a blessing. Please thank them for us."

"Wonderful, I'll pass on the message," Jorie added as she handed over the keys and an information card for the house. "I'll be back on Monday. If you need to talk before then, the nurses can reach me."

Meg

It didn't take long for Meg to settle in to room 14, a small, stark chamber consisting of nothing more than a bed, a table, and a chair. The single light bulb in the ceiling and the small window to the courtyard were both surrounded by metal bars, preventing the patient from having access to anything sharp. Meg was grateful to still have her iPod and headphones, as they provided the only source of escape from the tormented sounds echoing through the halls.

Detox was hell as far as she was concerned. Her body seemed to be in a constant state of sweat, panic, and sensory overload. In addition to that, she felt as if she were on a roller coaster, with her thoughts careening back and forth between wanting to escape and realizing there was nowhere to go.

She didn't understand why anyone had to care about her. She didn't. Why should they?

Perhaps they didn't know her very well, or they had an ulterior motive. Either way, she was certain she couldn't trust anyone.

So now, Meg figured she had a game to play, and play it she would. She needed to accept the role of an addict seeking recovery. Playing the part would get her out of here. Only then could she could finish the job she'd already messed up twice. Perhaps she'd try something more effective than an overdose next time.

The blaring music blocked out the sound of knocking on the door, and it wasn't until Jorie stood right in front of her that she realized she had company.

Meg greeted her with a fake smile while sliding as far away as possible into the corner of the bed. She surrounded herself with pillows in order to create a protective barrier between herself and the visitor. She'd been told the counselor would be the first person to visit. This woman would have access to her mind but not to her heart. *No one* was getting there again.

"Hello, Meg, I'm Jorie, one of the counselors here at the hospital. We met in the ER this morning."

"Hello," answered Meg quietly.

"Odd as this may sound, I need your help, and I hope we can work together while you're here. There are some things I need to let you know right away."

Here comes the fine print, Meg thought to herself as Jorie began. "Unless you state you're going to hurt yourself or others, what you share with me remains confidential, just between you and me. Now, if you *want* me to share information I can do so, but you'll need to sign a release of information to whomever you give me permission to share with.

"Believe it or not, my main work here in the hospital is to listen and help people feel good about themselves, empowering them to make changes when necessary. How do you feel about being here?"

"Great. I hope to get the help I need," Meg lied, purposely avoiding Jorie's gaze.

"Can I come sit next to you? I'd like to let you know what you can expect during your time here."

Meg nodded in agreement.

She put on her fake 'I'm listening' expression as Jorie got going. "Days two through five are going to be the toughest as your body readjusts to not having the drugs. There is some medicine to help you with the withdrawals. The doctor'll be here soon to go over the pros and cons of using it."

Meg winced at the realization that what she'd already experienced was not only going to get worse but would stay that way for what seemed like forever at this point.

"After the initial withdrawal, you'll still have cravings, but they won't be as strong," continued Jorie. "If you're doing well, and cooperating with the therapy, you'll be released within the next two weeks. Then, for two months, you'll need to return three times a week for group therapy as well as drug testing. At that point the therapy requirements drop to once a week and remain there for a year, as long as your drug tests remain negative. Any questions so far?"

Meg shook her head and hoped Jorie couldn't tell she'd zoned out after hearing about a release date. Details weren't necessary after that- in fact, the only thing she had to do was apologize to Jordan. Hopefully he'd be out of the hospital by the time she was released, but if not, she'd just get a note to one of his friends.

As if she could read Meg's mind, Jorie shifted gears. "Meg, all the stuff I've said so far might not mean much to you, but I really want you to listen now as this part just might."

After waiting long enough for Meg to clear her head, Jorie continued.

"Our program includes an alternative online high school component. As long as you're attending the therapy sessions and staying clean, you'll have a tremendous amount of support in getting your high school diploma. It's an accelerated program that allows us to remove two semesters worth of grades from your GPA, so in essence, you *could* graduate at the same time as your classmates with a GPA more in line with what you had before your struggles began. This is a fully accredited program recognized by most colleges, and could be the ticket to getting you back on track with the long term plans you once had."

Meg felt blindsided by the feelings of hope rising inside when she faintly remembered how proud she'd been of her perfect GPA. Her dreams of college, marriage, and a big family began flowing back towards a once prominent place in her heart.

But then, like a tsunami, other memories came rushing in, dragging along with them the sarcastic inner voice of condemnation. *Yeah right. You know better than to even consider those dreams again. Don't you remember what you did?*

"Meg, please share with me the thoughts you just had," Jorie implored, taking note of the changes in Meg's facial expression.

Quickly remembering her role, Meg lied. "Oh, I was just thinking about how that all sounds really good." Fearing that Jorie might dig deeper, she attempted to change the subject by asking, "How's Jordan doing?"

"I *will* share that with you, but first tell me how you know him," replied Jorie, realizing that so far *she'd* been doing nearly all the talking.

"He used to hang out with my-ex boyfriend, Toby. We double dated for the Christmas dance last year. They were on the wrestling team together until Toby got kicked off. Jordan was the only one who tried to help me when..." Meg caught herself before it was too late. "When... I needed help but thought I had it all figured out."

Meg noticed Jorie suppressing a smile and wondered why the news she'd just shared would make her happy.

"Jordan has serious burns and is in a coma. His parents will be spending every day with him, talking, reading, and inviting lots of company to visit." Jorie volunteered. "His chances of recovery are much better with lots of stimulation. The doctors don't know for sure if he can hear, and they can't even promise that he'll wake up, but everyone's going to do what they can to help."

"I met his parents the night of the Christmas dance last year," Meg willingly contributed. "They made us dinner, they were both really nice people. Could you ask his mom to come visit me?"

"I will when I see her on Monday," agreed Jorie. "Your first group session starts in fifteen minutes. After that, we'll have a chance to discuss the medications you may want to consider. Do you have any questions for me?"

"Do I have to talk today?"

"Nothing more than stating your name," Jorie answered with a smile. "Any other questions?"

Meg shook her head no.

"Okay, the nurse will stop by soon to show you where the session is. I'll see you there," Jorie stated while pressing the call button to let the desk attendant know she was ready to come out.

Paul

Paul gazed out the large picture window of Heather's private room at the skyline of downtown Philadelphia.

The streams of head- and tail lights snaking along the freeways and overpasses mesmerized him. The nearly full moon cast an eerie glow upon the thin veil of fog blanketing the cityscape, making it look like the opening scene of a horror movie.

Paul's reverie ended with the arrival of Heather's OB doctor.

"Well, young lady, weren't we just together this morning?" Dr. Brauer joked as he knocked on the door and then approached Heather's bed with an extended hand.

"Hi, Dr. Brauer. Yes, we were. I just figured you needed an added challenge before the weekend," Heather responded in a half-hearted attempt to match his humor.

"Well, you've certainly given me that. I heard about the accident. Thankfully you were pulled out when you were."

"Yes, it could have been *much* worse," interjected Paul, moving away from the window to join them. "We're really hoping the good fortune will continue."

"I'm joining you both in that hope," replied Dr. Brauer, extending his hand to greet Paul.

After examining the readings on the contraction monitor, Dr. Brauer delivered the treatment plan with cautious optimism.

"We know from this morning's appointment that your baby's development is right on track for 26 weeks. Your contractions have slowed since settling here, which is evidence that the bed rest and new medications are helping. We won't be checking your cervix unless the contractions begin to pick up."

"Every day we prevent you from going into labor is a victory. If she were born now, she'd have only a *slight* chance of survival. If you could hold off for two more weeks, her chances increase dramatically; however, it would still require her spending time in NICU. Our ultimate goal, of course, is for you to make it 11 more weeks, when she'd be considered full term, but for now let's just focus on getting to the two-week mark."

"Sounds like a plan," responded Heather, allowing herself to feel just a hint of hope for her child. "Aside from the medical treatment, is there anything else we can be doing?"

"I'm glad you asked," he said while checking the incline of her bed. "I can't emphasize enough the importance of your emotions. It's crucial that you both remain positive. I know that's quite a challenge, given your history of loss, however, it's best for everyone, especially the baby."

Heather and Paul nodded in agreement.

Dr. Brauer said his goodbyes and started out the door, nearly bumping into Jorie as she entered.

Jorie

Jorie, excited to be heading home after this visit, was happy to see that Heather's husband was still there. This was going to be another one of those tough long haul cases, she thought. It seemed she was getting more than the usual amount of them today.

"Hello, Heather. My name's Jorie Clayton. I was hoping to have a short visit if you're up for it."

"Sure am," answered Heather. "This is my husband Paul. You must be the counselor Rhonda mentioned."

"That I am. It's nice to meet both of you."

"Thanks, you too," added Paul.

Jorie prepared to make it a quick visit when she noticed Paul's nervous pacing and Heather's pale complexion.

"I was just visiting the parents of the young man who pulled you out of the car. They're very appreciative of the housing you two are providing and send their thank you's." she began.

Paul nodded in agreement as Heather replied, "it's the least we could do."

"So Heather, I understand you're 26 weeks along, you've had some contractions after the accident, and most likely will be on bed rest and medication for the remainder of your pregnancy."

"That sounds about right," she answered. We've lost three babies in the past and have never made it this far. At my appointment this morning, everything appeared normal and the baby was fine."

"What do you think is going to be the hardest part for you during this time?"

"Most definitely the isolation and lack of exercise. I'm normally quite active, so lying in bed ranks low on my list of priorities. However, I'm willing to do anything for our baby."

"And that's exactly what I'm here for. My role is to help you set up a schedule of activities, and be a sounding board for the feelings of frustration that are bound to show up."

"I'll leave you some questionnaires to look at over the weekend. Filling them out should help you remember things you've wanted to accomplish in the past but haven't taken the time to do. I'll be back on Monday to go over them with you and help you set up your schedule.

"Your job," Jorie added while turning towards Paul, "is to retrieve the materials needed for the activities. And also to visit as often as possible, since you'll be her main connection to the outside world."

"I'm happy to do so," replied Paul. "Thanks so much for your help."

"It's my pleasure. Unless you two have more questions, I'll be on my way."

"I do," replied Heather. "How are the two others injured in the accident? I heard the boy was life flighted, and the girl, are they alright?"

"Unfortunately I can't share that information, but I can say that they, like you, are going to be around for a while. Perhaps you'll have the chance to meet them."

"I hope I do. Thanks, Jorie, see you Monday," replied Heather, her voice exposing the state of exhaustion she was in.

Paul

As Paul struggled to find comfort in the bedside recliner, his thoughts wandered to Heather's previous miscarriages.

He remembered seeing her curled up in a ball, cradling her belly and crying herself to sleep in the tiny master bedroom of their first house. Her reaction was a surprise to him, as she'd only been two months along. She wasn't even showing, yet she'd announced the pregnancy to everyone. Now they had to share the bad news with each and every one of them.

Three years later they were hopeful when they passed the two-month mark, but that hope lasted only a short time. Fortunately, they'd only told a few close friends, so there wasn't as much explaining to do.

He remembered that shortly after the second one, Heather started avoiding those friends, most of whom had recently transitioned from one child to two. Paul still enjoyed their gatherings but realized it was hard for Heather, as the conversations always turned to their children.

They took extra precautions when the news came years later that they were once again expecting. Heather immediately discontinued her high-impact exercise routine, and spent most of her time sitting down. They hired a housekeeper, and Paul usually picked up dinner on his way home. Their guarded optimism as they reached the four-month mark evaporated in an instant with the arrival of the all-too-familiar signs of miscarriage.

Heather lost hope after the third one and wanted to consider adoption. Paul, however, was adamantly opposed to the idea, and when the subject came up would counter with an adoption horror story he'd heard.

Heather eventually realized the futility of her efforts and decided to turn the extra bedrooms into an exercise room and a guest room. As soon as the baby stuff was sold, she began pouring herself into her growing bookkeeping business.

Shortly before Heather's 40th birthday, Paul came across some research regarding new treatments for recurrent miscarriage. He noted the skepticism in Heather's voice as they discussed the news. She agreed to move forward on the condition that, if they were unsuccessful after a year or she miscarried again, they would adopt.

The doctor was puzzled by the couple's normal test results but continued with the standard treatment nevertheless. After a few months of fertility drugs, insemination was added to the treatment. Four disappointing months later their doctor suggested they move onto in vitro fertilization if the next treatment failed. That month the doctor brought in an acupuncturist as an added treatment.

The next round was a success; in fact, it was looking like the possibility of twins for a while. They'd continued with the acupuncture throughout the first trimester.

Though they seldom discussed it, Paul tried hard to suppress his excitement as 14 more weeks passed with no problems. Heather's phone call that very morning had been reassuring until the crash. He wondered when the sound of it would stop reverberating in his head.

Once he noticed Heather's rhythmic breathing, proof that she'd finally dozed off, Paul allowed himself to do the same.

The dream enveloped him like a fast-moving fog bank. He found himself sitting in a dilapidated swivel chair, his constant companion through four years of college and two years of grad school. Transitioning from school to his first job as a caseworker at a state-funded health center had gone smoothly. Most of his clients had been pretty much textbook cases; however, the one sitting in front of him now was anything but.

He noticed she smelled heavily of smoke and seemed incapable of sitting still, even for a moment. The mentally ill woman rambled on about a husband locking her out of the house, eventually sleeping under bridges, and feeling lucky to find some shelter in bushes by the river. She escaped from the father of her baby, and she had a new boyfriend she found while living at a nearby motel. She didn't want to get an abortion. This was a problem, since it was only after she was no longer pregnant that Paul could send her to a facility where she'd receive the necessary psychiatric care.

The methodical echo of a loose laundry cart wheel pulled him out of the dream and into the realization that his back felt like someone was taking a hacksaw to it. Although he was certain he'd be lonely, he was grateful that his next night would be spent at home. The thought of climbing into their luxurious king-size bed was exceptionally appealing at the moment.

Paul began to wonder about the young man who'd rescued his wife. Despite the obvious danger, he'd been willing to risk his life to save a stranger's. He pondered the idea of having a child of his own in the same situation and wondered if he'd want them to do the same.

4. A NEW WEEK

Jorie

Monday morning arrived without the usual crowded lobbies at Mercy Medical. Only the most critical services were being provided due to the ominous weather forecast.

The prospect of snow didn't slow Jorie down a bit. In fact, she loved the change of pace when snow fell. Complete strangers had something to talk about, neighbors checked in on each other, and her children received a day of unscheduled delight.

Sitting at her desk was something Jorie did only out of necessity. As far as she was concerned, it was simply an area to store the tools and information she needed to do what she loved best. In fact, if it weren't for the nearby window, she would most likely be there even less. Jorie had settled for only a moment to observe the large snowflakes linking up with each other before finding their place on the landscape, when the vibration of her phone startled her.

"I know you're a few minutes away from your appointment with Meg, but you may want to come a bit early. I have something I think you'll want to see," stated the on-duty nurse in the rehab wing.

Jorie grabbed her overflowing notebook, her coffee mug that was never quite full enough, and her phone, heading out the door at full speed.

The nurse had the video ready to go when Jorie arrived. On the screen they could see Meg asleep and apparently dreaming. The deep vertical lines on her forehead flashed in and out of view as her arms flailed wildly in front of her. She appeared to be moving things out of the way at a rapidly increasing rate, searching for something important.

It was impossible to fully understand what she was saying.

"Trying... I know... Almost there... Don't stop... I'm sorry, I'm sorry..." Meg's tormented voice trailed off as she flung her pillows across the room and curled up in a ball rocking to and fro.

"When I read about this in last night's notes," explained the nurse, "I rewound the recording and found the same thing occurred nearly every time she dozed off."

"Thank you. Can you forward it to me please?" Jorie asked.

"I can have it to you in five minutes."

"Thanks, I'm ready to go in now."

Jorie knocked gently as she entered Meg's room and moved towards the chair. "Hello, Meg, it's time for our appointment."

"Hi," Meg muttered as she removed her headphones and straightened her hair.

They chatted for a bit before Jorie got down to business.

"Meg, when you first came in to the ER, Wendy was pretty scared and upset. She told me she felt horrible about yelling at you. I know you don't want to see her, but would you be willing to hear something I asked her to write?

"Sure," answered Meg hesitantly.

"I asked her to write you a note explaining the reasons she was so angry. She gave me permission to share it with you," Jorie explained before reading the note out loud.

"I'm angry with you, Meg, because it seems like you've given up. You had so much going for you- good grades, lots of friends, plans for college. It's been hard to see you throw it all away. But worse than any of that is that you won't even talk to me. You mean so much to me and I'm afraid I've lost you forever. Please give me another chance. I love you, Wendy."

It was clear Meg was doing her best to not care as she listened to Wendy's words. Jorie gave her a moment to process what she'd heard before asking how it made her feel.

"Sad but not surprised," she answered with a pained expression. "I know she's right and I miss her too, but I'm not the same person anymore, and the sooner she accepts that, the better."

"Would you be willing to write your feelings in a response to her?" asked Jorie.

"I'll write it, but don't know if I want you to give it to her."

"Fair enough," Jorie conceded.

It was obvious from Meg's body language that it was time to move on to another subject.

"I spoke with your school counselor this morning, and they mentioned you had a drop in your grades right after the holidays last year; does that sound about right?"

"My grades tanked when I started getting high all the time; maybe we can blame it on that."

"So before then you only got high occasionally?"

"Only a few times before. I guess I used it for fun but never really *needed* it. But you know, stuff happens and life goes on, right?"

"Meg, I need you to know about some information the nurses have shared with me. They've noted that when you're asleep, they see and hear you crying and searching for something. What are your thoughts about this, and how do you feel being told that you've experienced it several times in just the last two days?"

"I don't know what to think about it. I don't remember my dreams, and I'm just too tired to figure it out."

"Would you be willing to watch a video clip of yourself having one of the dreams?"

"Yes, but I don't see why it'd do any good."

"Meg, I've been able to help many people with their addictions, and the first step has always been to figure out why they need them or, in other words, what they are running from. Sometimes while we're sleeping, our brain attempts to process stuff we have trouble facing when we're awake," Jorie replied as she pulled out her laptop and started the recording. "Now, as you're seeing this, I want you to imagine that it's someone else, not you- maybe someone you care about. Okay?"

Meg nodded in agreement and settled in to watch. Through tear-filled eyes, she saw herself frantically searching for something more precious than anyone could fathom. Remembering Jorie's suggestion, she was suddenly filled with deep compassion for the girl in the video.

"Can you share with me your feelings as you watch this?" Jorie asked gently.

"I feel sorry for her. She had an abortion and she's looking for her baby. She needs help, but I don't think she'll get it," whimpered Meg.

"Why can't she be helped?"

"Because it's *her* fault. She agreed to have the abortion, it was *her* choice, and now the dreams are *her* punishment," Meg declared, her voice teeming with judgment as she roughly scraped away the tears spilling from her eyes.

"Meg, as you're talking about this, your voice and facial expressions tell me you're angry. I want you to know it's *okay* to be angry. I don't know if you've heard that it's okay to have feelings, even if they're not *good* ones. Feelings are the way our hearts and guts communicate, like how thoughts are what our brain cells have communicated. Last week in the ER, you blamed Wendy for a ride sometime in the past. Was it to an abortion facility?"

Meg nodded.

"Meg, thank you for trusting me with this painful and private information. I've worked with many young women, some who have felt very angry and blamed themselves for having an abortion. These women are very strong, admirable, and think they can survive anything. I need to tell you about a lady I met a few years back, and *if* you're open to it, I'd love to have you meet her."

"I'm open to *hearing* about her," Meg agreed hesitantly.

"Her name's Liz. I met her at a garden I stumbled upon while visiting a lavender farm in the country. It's called the Garden of Hope. Liz was there pruning, and she told me and my mother that it was for memorializing children lost anytime after conception. It's beautiful and peaceful, with stone benches and several wooden posts covered with name plaques and short messages."

"She said some of the children were lost to miscarriages, some died shortly after birth, but the majority were children lost to abortion. Liz showed us a plaque with the name of a child she lost to abortion when she was 19. She said she suffered for many years until going through a healing program and that now she shares her story to encourage others to do the same."

"I can't believe there's a place like that and that someone could admit to a stranger they'd had an abortion," Meg confided, almost as if it were too good to be true and too horrible to imagine all at the same time.

Like a dam developing a fast-flowing leak, it appeared to Jorie that Meg was struggling to contain her emotions.

"So you'll meet with her?" asked Jorie hopefully, holding out a box of kleenex.

"Yes, I'll meet with her," Meg agreed. "It looks like I have to do *something;* seems like the only other option is death, and I can't even seem to get that right!" she added with a reserved smile.

"Awesome, I'll call her today. I'm so excited for you, Meg. Thank you for trusting me; it means a lot."

Jorie could barely contain her excitement as she said goodbye to Meg. They'd made tremendous progress in a short time. It was sessions like this that made up for the heartbreak she felt when she failed to give her clients the hope they needed in order to hold on.

Trevor

"Good morning, son, it's going to be a wonderful day," declared Trevor, sailing into Jordan's room early Monday morning lugging a box full of posters, a bulletin board, and a small set of speakers. The guitar strapped to his back, having barely survived the journey, was swinging side to side and nearly crashed into the door frame as he entered.

Karina followed close behind, carrying two large bags of supplies.

Trevor watched her set down the bags, open the blinds, and give Jordan a quick kiss on the forehead. She picked a wet yellow leaf off of her coat before hanging it neatly in the closet.

"Hey, Trev, would you mind setting up the sound system before you head out?" she asked in a voice he had trouble saying 'no' to.

"No prob; I'll put these posters up, too. The storm's hitting soon, so I'll need to take off pretty quick. I'll drop your suitcase off at the guesthouse on my way out of town."

"Awesome. I don't know what we'd have done without the use of that house," Karina added.

"Well, the way I figure, you'd have moved in right here with Jordan, sleeping in this lovely recliner. So yes, having use of the house *is* pretty wonderful," he chuckled while starting in on his tasks.

Glancing out the window a short time later, Trevor noticed the last remaining leaves being stripped from the branches by the inconsistent gusts of east wind. "Winds are picking up, looks like the storm's arriving right on time," he said reluctantly. "Headin' out now. Jordan, you take care of your mom and don't get into too much trouble. I'll see you in a few days," Trevor promised as he gently ruffled what was now showing of his son's thick black hair. The bandages wrapping his entire head had been traded for a much smaller one covering only the injured area on the back.

Walking out, he fondly remembered the last time they wrestled. It was an important match in Liz's kitchen, with the last of her cream puffs awaiting the victor. There had been no doubt who'd be enjoying it. It had been years since Trevor even stood a chance against Jordan.

"I'll call you when I'm back at the farm," Trevor promised as he and Karina walked to the elevator. After a longer than usual hug, he slid through the closing doors and pushed the button for the lobby. Watching the lighted floor numbers consistently decreasing, he contemplated how unsettling it was to be headed home without his wife.

Karina

Karina took a deep breath, lifted her head high, and reminded herself she *could* do this. It was encouraging to enter Jordan's room for the second time today and see the dramatic difference made by their decorating efforts.

Though it seemed strange at first, she quickly became accustomed to their one-sided conversations.

"Hey, hon, you're probably gonna get sick of hearing my voice, but we're gonna keep things hoppin' in here, unless you wake up and tell us to leave you alone," she chuckled. "And don't worry, you *will* be hearing voices besides mine. In fact, we have a calendar set up so you'll be having company most every day. You have an awful lot of people who love and want to visit you.

"Your guitar's in the corner, your posters are on the wall and right here near the bed are photos of your football team and your crazy family. And guess what? You managed to win Homecoming King without even being there! The vote was already in when you... oh, wait. I guess I'd better start at the beginning, just in case you're wondering what happened.

"Today's Monday. Last Friday you were headed to school for the coronation practice. You stopped at the scene of an accident and pulled a pregnant woman out of her burning car just before it exploded. You shielded them, and as a result, took the full brunt of it.

"Oh, honey, you have lots of burns on your back, and your head was injured, which is why you're in a coma. Since there's a chance you can hear us, and we have no way of knowing, we're going to assume you can.

"Your team won 42-19, and the coronation was a first of its kind. They made a life-sized cardboard cut-out of you and held it up in your place. I heard that when your cut-out was crowned, the crowd first cheered and then had a moment of silence in your honor. Amalia was crowned queen, which I'm sure wouldn't surprise you. She didn't want to go to the dance without her best guy friend, but everyone insisted and made her do it anyway.

"So many of your friends want to come see you, but we're keeping it family only this week. I'm gonna read a few of the messages on your Facebook wall. This first one's from Eli."

"'Bro! It's amazing what lengths you'll go to in order to get out of a dance! I know you don't like em' dude- but really? Get better soon, we miss you around here!'"

"Juan says, 'Jordan, just so you know, even when you're in a coma, you're still my hero!'"

"Kyle says, 'Oh no! Who's gonna feed me now? Come home sooooon!'"

"Ramon says something in Spanish and then in English says, 'You're just gonna have to figure that one out! Miss you friend.'"

"And Nick says, 'You know Jordan, this really sucks. It was funny that the girls were lined up waiting to dance with your cut-out, which by the way, I think looks better than you do! Haha.'"

A gentle tapping at the door came as a welcome interruption, since the growing lump in Karina's throat was making it difficult to continue.

"Hi, Karina, can I speak with you out here for a moment please?" she heard Jorie ask from the hall.

"Sure, be right out," she replied before pushing "play" on the iPod. "Okay, Jordan, I'll be back in a bit, hope you enjoy the playlist Lidya made for you. She said it reminded her of the time you stayed home just to keep her company when she had chickenpox."

Settling into their seats, Karina was more than willing to accept the steaming latte offered up by this woman she hoped to get to know better.

"How's it going so far?" inquired Jorie.

"Well, as I've nothing to compare it with, I'd say pretty good. It seems awkward carrying on the one-sided conversations, but it helps to imagine how he'd be responding if he could."

"That's a great way to look at it. I believe the hardest part for you is going to be dealing with the isolation. I suggest you leave the room every couple of hours, get to know some people around the hospital, or just go to the cafeteria for a change of scenery. There's a nice park two blocks south of here with a walking path around the perimeter. I like to go there for my lunch breaks. My favorite coffee shop is just one block past the house you're staying in. They have wonderful muffins and even the day-old ones are still delicious."

"Thanks for the ideas. I'll check out the park during lunch today. I can't tell you how much it means to have a room to stay in right near the hospital. Please let the couple know how much we appreciate their gift. How are *they* doing?"

"They're hanging in there. Heather will be here for the remainder of her pregnancy. Perhaps you could stop in and thank her yourself."

"I think I'll do that," replied Karina. "And what about the young lady, how is she?"

"I'm glad you asked, because there's something you could do that might help her. She knows your son, and learning he's in serious condition has really affected her. She says she's met you as well. Her name is Meg Kirkwood."

"Oh, yes, we fixed dinner for her and her boyfriend before a dance last year. They doubled with Jordan and his date. I remember her as smart, outgoing, full of energy, and very pretty. Are her injuries serious?"

"*Physically,* no. But I'm trying to figure out why the girl that's here is not the same one you just described. Only then can I help her. She's refusing to see her family but *is* open to a visit from you. She has questions about Jordan that I can't answer- perhaps you can."

"Where will I find her?" asked Karina without hesitation.

"She's in room 14 of the rehab wing. I'll put your name on the list of those who can visit. You'll just need to show your ID at the reception desk. Thank you so much."

After saying their goodbyes, Karina returned to Jordan's room just in time for the highlight of her day.

"Hey, we heard there was a party in here!" shouted Lidya, Jordan's youngest sister, as she and his four other siblings came flooding into the room. Karina greeted each of her children with a hug and spent some time catching up on the happenings of their weekend. Assuming they'd have no trouble keeping the conversation going, she decided to head out and do some visiting of her own.

The rehab wing was at the opposite end of the hospital from Jordan's room. Karina, remembering Jorie's advice, grabbed her coat so she could take the longer outdoor route through the courtyard. The winds, having completed their job of rendering the trees naked, now provided simple delight to Karina. A unique display of swirling leaves mixed with the falling snow fluttered around her.

Pulling the ID out of her wallet at the reception desk, Karina felt grateful she wasn't visiting one of her children here. She was escorted to Meg's room and was informed that when it was time to leave, she just needed to press the call button.

Meg was sitting on her bed, once again wedged into the corner with the pillows. She was half sleeping, half awake, listening to music. The pale, gaunt face looked nothing like the one she'd seen less than a year ago. In fact, Karina was certain she would've never made the connection on her own.

When Meg saw Karina, she quickly sat up, removed her earplugs, and straightened her hair.

"I'm surprised you came," she commented at a volume barely loud enough to hear.

"I'm happy to do so," replied Karina. "Is it alright if I sit down?"

"Yes. Do you remember me?" asked Meg.

"Of course I do; we enjoyed getting to know you last year. We haven't had the chance to meet many of Jordan's high school friends. Having him move here has been great for him, but we've missed him terribly."

Meg gazed right at her but failed to respond.

Not wanting to discuss Meg's current condition until she was ready, Karina decided to keep the conversation surface-level. "Have you noticed that all the leaves came off this morning?" she asked, gesturing towards the small window.

Glancing slowly towards the window and back again, Meg responded flatly, "Haven't really cared about the seasons for a while now."

Karina wondered what could have happened- it appeared as if the life had been sucked out of this once vivacious young lady. Realizing that small talk was *not* what Meg had asked her here for, Karina simply asked, "What would you like to talk about, Meg?"

"Mrs. Parrish, I'm sorry that I caused the accident. I didn't want to hurt anyone. Well, except myself, and of everyone I know, Jordan is the *last* person that deserves to be here."

"First of all, please call me Karina, and to be honest I thought your sister was driving. Why do you feel you're to blame?"

"I caused the accident. My sister ran the stop sign when she saw how sick I was from the pills I took. I tried to kill myself, but I never wanted to hurt Jordan," cried Meg, her tears dropping onto the pillows. "I'm so sorry," she whispered with her head hanging low.

"Meg, I'm not angry with you *or* your sister. And although I never want harm to come to my son, I'm proud of him for saving two lives, even at the risk-"

"*One* life!" corrected Meg defensively, her head snapping up and her eyes boring straight into Karina.

Sensing this was an extremely sensitive issue, Karina leaned back in her chair and waited patiently for Meg to relax.

It was clear Meg was embarrassed by her venomous response, but Karina was not one to hold grudges. Meg seemed conflicted, almost like she couldn't decide whether she wanted to continue the conversation.

"I'm sorry again, please forgive me," Meg pleaded.

"No problem," Karina answered with compassion. "However, I do need to respond to your comment, if you're willing to listen."

"Yes," whispered Meg.

"The way I see it it's pretty simple. There were two hearts beating in that car before the accident happened. If Jordan hadn't pulled her out, those two hearts would have stopped," she explained gently. " By that reasoning, he saved the lives of two people, the mother and her baby."

"I've never thought of it like that," replied Meg pensively.

"Jordan was rescued when he was still inside *his* mother," continued Karina. "He was saved by many people, but it started with a stranger. He knows that, and he's been taught to believe that *every* life is valuable, regardless of size or age."

"True, that is something I *do* know about him," concurred Meg.

"How much longer will you be in here?" asked Karina.

"I've heard a couple of weeks if I cooperate, then I need to come back three times a week for therapy," replied Meg.

"Well, Meg, I really hope you *do* cooperate. I'd love to see you get healthy and back on track towards that amazing future you described last year. I can't stay long today, just wanted to stop by and wish you well. I plan on being around for weeks or maybe even longer. Is it alright if I visit again? I'd love to chat more if you're up for it."

"Are you sure you want to?" asked Meg suspiciously.

"You'd be helping *me,* Meg. I'll be needing a break from Jordan's room, and I'm happy to come visit."

"Okay then, thank you, Karina," Meg said shyly as she stood up to say goodbye.

Meg

Reflecting back over the conversation, Meg pondered how odd it was that she could be both hopeful and agitated at the same time. She was pleased to have remained in the conversation even after becoming angry. Jordan was different than all her friends. He had something they didn't and she felt compelled to find out exactly what that was.

Karina seemed like someone she could trust, who, like Jordan, truly cared about others. It was the debate about the number of people in the car that bothered her the most.

Why did she have to make the point about the heartbeat of the baby? Didn't she know how frustrating that was? It would be so much easier if everyone just used the same terminology and reasoning. Fetus instead of baby, or blob of tissue instead of a child. The woman can always have another one. It's good that Jordan rescued her, but why all the fuss over her being pregnant?

Her mind once again began racing uncontrollably with conflicting emotions, which made her long for the familiar numbness she knew could be achieved with drugs. It didn't matter which kind it was: Vicodin, OxyContin, Percocet, Xanax, Valium, Adderall or Ritalin- they all did the job. Just a few pills, only enough to take the edge off and quiet her mind. Cranking her music to the highest volume possible, and adjusting the earphones, Meg's only hope of escape was to fall asleep.

Heather

"Oh, hi, Jorie! You have perfect timing. I just finished my homework," Heather said with an air of accomplishment as Jorie entered the room.

"Awesome, let's hear what you have planned."

"I may be biting off more than I can chew, which would be nothing new, but I'd like to learn a new language, crochet, start a blog, organize recipe files, organize photos, and read some books. I have a friend taking over my bookkeeping business until I'm ready to return."

"This is a great list," Jorie replied. "If you don't already have a language program, I recommend Rosetta Stone. You can order yarn and crochet directions online as well. Your next assignment is to set up a daily schedule from eight to five, with every hour being planned out. We can go over it tomorrow. I'm happy to hear your contractions are under control and can imagine you are as well."

"Yep, I'm feeling good and concentrating on staying positive."

"Very promising to hear. Is there anything I can do or get for you right now?" Jorie asked.

"No, but thanks for your help. The whole thing seems more bearable now."

They said their goodbyes and Heather had just settled in to work on her schedule when she received a call.

"Hi ,hon, how's it going so far today?" Paul asked.

"Great. The contractions have stopped completely, and I've got a long list of activities planned."

"Wonderful," he replied. "I need to go into a meeting now, I'll see you this evening. Save room for your favorite Thai food."

"Yum! See you tonight," she replied while looking over at her barely-touched breakfast and imagining the promised cuisine in its place.

"Hello!" chimed Karina, poking her head in the doorway. "Are you up for a visit?"

"More than you can imagine," replied Heather, wondering if this might be the other hospital counselor. "Bed rest isn't as wonderful as it sounds."

"Great. I'm Karina Parrish. My son Jordan pulled you out of the car," she said while striding in and offering her hand in greeting.

"Oh, Karina, it's really nice to meet you. I'm Heather, please sit down. There are no words to express how grateful we are to your son. He's truly our hero."

"Thanks, we're really proud of him. His life's been a miracle from the beginning and just continues to amaze us," Karina replied, her words coated with raw emotion.

"Thank *you* for the gift of housing during his hospital stay," she continued. "We really appreciate having a home base close by, since we live nearly two hours away in Garden View. My husband Trevor and I will be trading places on the weekends."

"We're more than happy to help; in fact, it's the least we can do. I can't imagine being separated from our little girl when she needed us," Heather answered softly, placing one hand on her belly.

"Do you have other children as well?" asked Karina.

"No. Well, we lost three to miscarriage," answered Heather cautiously.

"Ahhh, I'm sorry for your many losses."

"Thanks, it's refreshing to have someone respond that way. So many well-intending people end up invalidating their short lives, but my heart knows otherwise. How about you? Is Jordan your only child?"

"No, we have six total, four biological and two adopted; in fact, they're all in Jordan's room right now. It's pretty crazy in there," Karina chuckled. "Have you chosen a name for your little girl?"

"Not yet, but we hope to soon. Was Jordan adopted?" asked Heather, wondering why she was able to connect with this mother of many. Usually the pain was too great.

"Yes, he's number four in the line-up, born six weeks after the birth of number three, so, in a sense, we have twins. It really confuses people, because Jordan has jet black hair and his same-age brother has blonde."

"You're kidding. I'd love to hear more about that, but first I really want to know how he's doing."

"He's burned pretty badly, but the worst part is he suffered head trauma and is in a coma. We're trying to provide lots of stimulation to increase his odds of recovery."

Karina tilted her ear towards the door and smiled broadly. The sound of laughter, singing, and guitar music had been steadily increasing and now filled the hallway.

"I'd love to visit with you more, but it'll have to be at another time, since it sounds like my children are taking that stimulation challenge a little too far," she chuckled. "Why don't you see about coming down to Jordan's room sometime? It'd be a change of scenery for you, and I'd love the company."

"What a great idea, I'll ask. Thanks for the invite and the visit. You really brightened my day!" chimed Heather.

Karina

"Mine, too," replied Karina as she waved goodbye, excited to be returning to Jordan.

Passing the nurses' station along the way, Karina noticed several were tapping their feet, keeping time with the rhythm. Most were smiling and seemed to be enjoying the energy flowing out of Jordan's room. One of the nurses made eye contact with Karina, noticed her apologetic demeanor, and implored with a smile, "Please don't make them stop; we love it!"

As she joined her children, Karina was struck by the contrast of this room versus the two she'd just been in.

Meg's room was steeped with anger, bitterness, and loss of hope. Heather's seemed to be in a state of longing, with empty arms aching to be filled. This one, however, was overflowing with love and life and a presence of joy despite the challenges within. History had proven that this family grew closer during the storms of life and she was overwhelmed with gratitude for the privilege of mothering every one of her children.

Laurelle, the oldest at 24, stood in the far corner strumming the guitar and singing, while Stoller, next in line at 22, sat near Jordan reading a book of silly jokes. Davian, also 18, and Ruth, two years younger, were immersed in a rivalrous game of cards. Lidya, the youngest at 13 and also adopted, sat near the door sketching the entire scene. What Karina was *unable* to see, due to a blanket covering his hand, was Jordan's index finger pulsing ever so slightly in an attempt to keep time with the music.

After saying goodbye to all but one of her children, Karina realized she was exhausted and had no problem dozing off while watching the bare tree branches accepting their first blanket of snow for the season.

Jorie

The first thing Jorie noticed upon entering Jordan's room was that, with the exception of the hospital bed, it looked no different than any other teenager's bedroom. It was obvious Jordan's parents were following her advice. She'd heard from the nurses that it'd been boisterous earlier that day, and was assured that they as well as neighboring patients, enjoyed it immensely.

"Knock knock," she whispered, noting that Karina had been napping.

"Oh, hello" she answered in a raspy voice.

"Hi, Karina. Rumor has it there was quite a party in here today."

"Yep, that's usually the case when *all* our children get together."

"Well, it's too bad they can't come every day then. It sounds like they did an excellent job of keeping this room full of stimulation."

"Thanks. As much as I'm saddened by the reason we're here, I do have to admit that it's nice being with him so much lately. We've missed Jordan at home these last few years."

"Where's he been living?" Jorie asked.

"He moved in with family friends, so he could wrestle at Central High. They have a much more developed program than our school back home. He had full ride offers from several colleges. It's amazing how fast plans can change, isn't it?"

"Sure is, seems as if life seldom turns out like we've planned. I've found that the happiest people are those willing and able to adapt and make the best of what comes their way."

"I couldn't agree more," added Karina. "By the way, I visited both Meg and Heather today. It was shocking to see the changes in Meg since I first met her. We chatted for a while and she agreed to see me again. She seems to have been hurt pretty bad."

"Good to know. Yes, Meg is hurting, but I'm optimistic we'll be able to help her. Thank you for reaching out. Now, what I'm here to find out is how are *you* doing, Karina?"

"Well, It's hard being away from home. At the same time, I can't imagine being anywhere else. This waiting reminds me of before Jordan was born. There were so many times we didn't know if he was going to survive."

"I see in his files he's adopted. You must have had contact with his birth mother during the pregnancy?"

"Yes; in fact Eva lived with us for several months before he was born. It was extremely difficult for everyone, especially her, but it was our only option at the time."

"How'd you meet her?"

"We found her through the lady Jordan's been living with. She was helping Eva with housing, food, and emotional support. Perhaps you'll get to meet Liz, since she'll be coming several times a week to spend time with Jordan and give me breaks."

"I'd love to meet her, and I'm happy to hear you'll be getting breaks; that's really important. I'll be stopping by to check in every day, and you have my number if you need me sooner," Jorie said before saying her goodbyes and continuing her rounds.

Shortly after leaving the room, she collided head on with a smiling silver-haired woman deliberately blocking her path.

"Liz!" Jorie shouted while giving her friend a heartfelt hug. "I haven't seen you in person for three years. I just left you a message; what are you doing here?"

"I'm here to help a friend whose son's in a coma. It looks like you and I might get to sneak in some visits, since I'm planning to be here often," replied Liz.

Jorie's mind raced back over her recent conversation with Karina, and the pieces quickly settled into place.

Had twenty years really passed since they'd first met at the garden? She recalled a few years later hearing about a homeless, mentally ill woman Liz was helping and had been relieved to hear the baby was adopted by an amazing couple that lived on a dairy farm.

"Oh my God! So *Jordan* is the child born to the homeless woman you helped. I was just in his room!" Jorie proclaimed.

"He sure is," Liz beamed. "It's been such a joy watching him grow, knowing I got to play a small part in the miracle."

"Wow. Yes, we *will* have to get together for coffee. This is amazing. On another note, I just left you a message regarding a young lady in our drug rehab wing. Her name's Meg, she's a senior in high school, and her life went into a tailspin last year. She just opened up about it this morning, and I think she'd benefit from some time with you. I told her just a little about you and she agreed to a visit. Do you have time today?"

"Sure, I'll stop by after my visit with Jordan. Please text me her room number. It's so good to see you," Liz said as they hugged goodbye and continued their separate ways.

Liz

Standing in the doorway to Jordan's room, Liz paused to hear the one-way conversation while Karina recanted in great detail the news from home.

"Thirty-two of the cows broke through the fence yesterday. It took your dad and three farm hands most of the morning to collect them. They were unaware until Mrs. Jacobs called, telling us six of them were feasting in her newly planted garden. And your little sister was awarded the sportsmanship award at the soccer banquet last night."

"Hello, dear! I just love to hear the news from home," exclaimed Liz as she entered, set down her backpack, and gave Karina a long hug.

"Hi Liz, thanks so much for coming! I've been talking so much lately, my voice is starting to go."

"This room is so full of love, I could even feel it from down the hall," Liz commented. "I ran into my friend Jorie, she's a counselor on staff. You know her, right?"

"Yeah, she was just here. I was telling her how much I wanted you two to meet! How do you know her?" asked Karina.

"We met quite a few years ago at the Garden of Hope, before I met you, in fact. She and her mom showed up while I was there pruning. We've been in touch ever since. She refers her clients to me occasionally. How's our young man doing today?"

"About the same," answered Karina, looking over at Jordan. "The burns are starting to heal already. It's hard to say how long this journey will be. I like to believe he can hear us; it makes it easier to keep rambling on with no response."

"We had a great conversation over breakfast a few weeks back," Liz shared. "He was nervous about his tattoo appointment, excited about the upcoming homecoming game, and not too thrilled about the dance. I asked if he was getting closer to a decision on college. Berkeley was at the top of the list. He said he really liked the coach and they had the highest law school acceptance rate."

"Yeah, he'd informed me about the tattoo, the game and the dance. But that's the first I've heard about the interest in law, though it doesn't surprise me," replied Karina. "A few years ago he was asking questions about the legal organization that offered to represent you while you were supporting Eva. He certainly has a passion for helping people, which is exactly why we're all here right now, isn't it?" she chuckled half-heartedly.

"Yes, it is," Liz agreed somberly. "I'm having trouble accepting this happened to him."

"We are, too. But we all know that if he survives, he'll find a way to make the best of it. It just may take awhile. "

"So very true," agreed Liz. "Now I hope you have somewhere to go while I'm covering for you."

"Yes, I'm gonna visit some other patients and get a few moments of fresh air," Karina replied.

"Awesome, you be sure and be gone for at least two hours, okay? We'll be keeping busy while you're away," Liz insisted as she ushered Karina to the door.

Normally, it seemed as if time went too fast when she was with any of her children. Liz had given birth to four, helped raise several including Jordan, and lost one before birth. But this scenario was far from normal, and keeping things lively for the next two hours was going to be a challenge. Fortunately, challenges were nothing new to Liz so she dove in head first.

"So Jordan, what do you wanna talk about?" she began. "Favorite things? Cool! You've been living with us long enough that I've got a good chance at guessing yours. I'll go first. Color? I'm sure yours is green. Mine is purple of course, any shade.

"Food? For you I'm gonna say buckwheat waffles, bacon, strawberry milkshakes, and lasagna. Myself on the other hand, it's just about impossible to have too much shrimp, avocado, salmon, or chocolate.

"Cars? I'm pretty sure it would be a black Jeep, with a soft top and a bike rack on the back for you. Always a Subaru for me please, any color except white.

"Time of year? There is no doubt about it for you- wrestling season. But then again, it could also be summer. I know you love being back on the farm."

"I can talk forever about my favorite time of the year. It's the first week of August, which we always spend at the coast. We started vacationing near Raritan Bay back in '92."

Liz leaned back in the recliner and closed her eyes. She could feel the salty air rolling in with the afternoon fog and filling her lungs ,as her spirit flooded with 36 years of memories. Even the not-so-good memories were remembered with fondness after time had a chance to soften them.

"In the beginning we camped with several other families and had a blast boogie boarding, riding biks, and eating lots of crab and marshmallows around the fire."

"Charles would spend most days on the bay with anyone from the group who wanted to help pull in the crab pots. Then several of the nights we'd have a potluck centered around the catch for the day."

"Eventually we transitioned into renting a huge old Cape Cod-style house with a wrap-around deck facing the bay. It's kid and dog-friendly, which means it's already pretty beat up, so we don't have to worry about it. The floors are not level, which only adds to the charm. We spend the whole week hanging out, playing in the sand, eating nonstop, watching movies, and crabbing.

"Now, I love reading books to the grandchildren and sharing funny stories about their parents when they were little. The grandchildren insist on hearing the same ones every year.

"Lee's birthday often fell during our trip, and one year her favorite gift was a large set of Nancy Drew books. In hindsight we wondered if it was such a good gift idea because for the remainder of the week, we hardly even saw her.

"One year Carol was relaxing in the front seat of the minivan, with her legs propped up on the dashboard. She was in her teens, and her legs were so long that when she stretched them out, she actually broke the windshield.

"And there was the time Renee, a barely-walking toddler, was playing in a bucket of freshly caught clams. One of them closed on her pinky finger, and she screamed for what seemed like hours but was really only a few minutes. When the clam was finally broken off with a ballpoint pen, the end of her finger was flat. Fortunately it didn't stay that way for long. The grandchildren always laugh when I imitate our friend who was running around screaming hysterically, 'The clams got the baby!'

"When Newman was around six, he went to a presentation put on by the camp rangers and decided to join the elite group of campers dubbed *Junior Rangers.* Taking his role quite seriously, he spent the remainder of the week diligently enforcing the safety rules of the campground, much to both the amusement and annoyance of the rest of us.

"And the favorite story of all is when it rained so hard Uncle Jed dug a trench around his family's tent. The kids were thrilled when they woke the next day to find a family of rubber ducks floating in it.

"Our older grandchildren have heard the stories so many times that, if I don't tell it exactly as before, they're quick to point it out.

"After the rubber ducky story, I always present the grandchildren with rubber ducks of their own. Next on the agenda is a trip to the beach to make a gigantic sand castle. Of course, it's imperative that the castle have a large moat for the ducks."

Liz adored her grandchildren, but occasionally the joy she experienced when they were with her was peppered with sorrow. It was impossible to ignore the realization of the little ones who might have been, had she chosen differently.

Over the years, she'd learned that when these sad feelings surface, it's important to remember the good things that came as a result of her loss, and one of them was right in front of her.

"You know when I first met your birth mom," Liz continued, "I learned quickly how clear she was about her likes and dislikes. The first time I took her out to breakfast, she doused her hash browns with about a half cup of ketchup. I commented that she must really like ketchup and she replied with, 'no, I just really hate hash browns'."

"I'm so happy her condition's improved since those days. It broke my heart to hear about the many unattainable desires she had. She loved animals but was unable to care for them, she wanted to work but struggled with social interaction, and she wanted to find a man who stuck around because of *her* rather than the monthly check she received. She wanted to take college classes and learn to drive and to cook, but more than anything she wanted to keep you, Jordan. She loves you immensely but was afraid she might hurt you. It made her feel better when I assured her that many women could be your mother, but only she could give you life."

Liz looked over at Jordan's large hand and recalled how tiny his fingers were the day he was born. One of her favorite photos from that day was of his little hand cradled in Eva's. Her nails were short, the black nail polish slightly chipped. Just the way her hand gently touched his conveyed her deep longing for him.

She and Charles enjoyed having Jordan live with them. It was fun having a young one in the home again and when their grandchildren visited, they adored tackling him. *It's really the little things that matter the most,* she thought.

Grabbing one of the books to read aloud, Liz decided to start at the beginning so she'd get the whole story. She knew Jordan would understand.

Hours later, winding through the meandering courtyard path on her way to meet Meg, Liz made a mental note to add an extra layer the next time she left home. Liz loved the changing of the seasons. This wasn't always the case, however, and for many years fall had delivered only sadness. It was difficult to enjoy the season when her body remembered things her mind was working frantically to forget.

But those years were long gone and now the season escorted in many happy memories: the births of several children and grandchildren, 44 wedding anniversaries with her best friend, and the thrill of completing a 683 mile ministry walk around the state when she was younger.

Liz welcomed the rush of warm air as she reentered the hospital and approached the rehab wing reception desk.

"I'll need to see your ID after you sign in please," stated the man behind the counter. "And you'll need to leave your backpack here."

Her footsteps echoed down the long, colorless hallway as she followed the volunteer escort. It was clear that anyone trying to escape would have a difficult time.

Before she knew it, "You can check out any time you like, but you can never leave", a line from the song "Hotel California", was playing in her head.

Meg

Meg was staring at the dropped ceiling panels, looking for patterns that looked like constellations, when the door opened and a woman she didn't know walked in.

"Hello, Meg, I'm Liz. Jorie asked me to stop by for a visit. Is now a good time?" she asked.

"Sure, I'm surprised you came so quickly," Meg replied from the well worn corner of the bed.

"Well, I was already here for a visit when I ran into Jorie," Liz replied, making herself comfortable in the nearby chair.

"Thanks for coming, but I'm not sure it's gonna be worth your time."

"It's always worth my time if you're willing to listen," replied Liz gently. "How much did Jorie tell you about me?"

"That you met at a garden, showed her a plaque for your child, and said that lots of people have problems after an..." Her voice trailed off, unable to form the word.

"How about I just share with you the big picture and then you can ask any questions you have?" Liz suggested.

Meg nodded in agreement and Liz began.

"I was barely 19 when I got my abortion. Afterwards I started drinking and smoking a lot of pot when before I'd only done it occasionally for fun. When I got married a few years later, I quit smoking and slowed way down on drinking, which made it so I thought about my abortion more often. I had a lot of problems with anger. When I got pregnant again, I assumed things would get better, but instead they got worse. As we had more children over the years, I could never justify what I'd done. I had trouble bonding with my children. I couldn't trust my husband and we almost divorced. I suffered with many emotional problems for 17 years before I went through a healing program that helped me process my feelings and let go of the anger I'd been holding onto. After that I was able to start putting my life back together. Since then I've been sharing my story one-on-one and publicly, encouraging others to find healing. And that's why I'm here. I'm hoping you'll have some questions and that through this you'll feel some hope that things could be better for you."

Meg moved the hair away from her face and adjusted the pillows around her before asking, "Where were you living?"

"I'd just finished my freshman year of college and had to take a year off so I'd qualify for a grant. I lived at a motel, cleaning rooms in exchange for one of my own. I was working two other jobs as well, making sandwiches at a deli during the day and waiting tables at a steakhouse at night."

"How'd you find out you were pregnant?"

"I'd just broken up with a guy I'd been dating for months when an old boyfriend called. Ben was getting ready to head back to college and wanted to take me out. I still adored him. He was smart, funny, cute. Seeing him again had me on cloud nine. There'd been opportunities in the past, but we'd always stopped short of having sex. We went out to dinner, then went dancing and had a few drinks. This time there was no stopping. Weeks later, I sat by myself in an exam room. A nurse came in, told me I was pregnant, and handed me a piece of paper with an address. She said, 'This is where you can go to get it taken care of.'"

It was hard to imagine this woman being her age, however, as Meg listened, it seemed as if Liz's gray hair and wrinkles simply disappeared.

"It was late on a Friday afternoon, and I remember the parking lot being nearly empty when I went out. I'll never forget that moment. Leaves had been falling all day and there were empty patches where cars had been parked. I remember sitting in my car and thinking to myself, 'I need to decide if I want to be a mother'. What I didn't know then was that I already *was* one."

"Who'd you tell first?" asked Meg, moving to the edge of the bed to be closer.

"My coworker Michelle and I had plans to celebrate my birthday weekend in Canada. I don't remember how I told her, but I know it was on the way. I recall her saying she'd had two abortions and they were no big deal."

"Did you tell the father?" Meg asked.

"Meg, what I'm going to share exposes my dishonesty not only with myself but with others as well. It's embarrassing to admit, but an important part of my healing was to face all of the pressures I felt at the time, and the thoughts I went through while making my decision. Are you doing okay? Is this too much for you right now?"

Meg was so engrossed in the story that it took a moment to respond. "No, Liz, it's not too much. Please keep going," she implored.

"The long drive gave me lots of time to think. It was raining and we had our favorite tape playing on the stereo. Because I'd had sex with two guys since my last period, I wasn't positive who the father was. However, the contrast between the two made it very easy to convince myself who I most *wanted* it to be.

"Cameron worked only occasionally and was heavy into injectible steroids for bodybuilding. He wasn't someone I'd consider spending my life with, but I was incredibly lonely. My family had blown apart when my parents divorced, I felt as if I didn't belong anywhere, and I was settling for anyone who showed me affection. Ben on the other hand was in college, and had a bright future. He was healthy, getting good grades, and played college baseball. It was from a bar in Canada that I made the first phone call to Ben."

"The music from the band blared throughout the whole building. I'll never forget standing in the dark, smoky hallway yelling into that big black plastic payphone handset. 'I'm calling to let you know I'm pregnant,' I said."

"His heavy sigh sounded like a hurricane coming through the line. 'I'm not ready to be a father,' he said after a long pause. 'Okay' I answered, trying to disguise the feeling that a very sharp knife had just sliced through my heart. I took his response as a complete rejection. It felt as if everything I was -my heart, soul and body- was simply tossed aside. "

"After another long pause I heard, 'Have you considered adoption? You know, my dad was adopted.'"

"'Don't know yet, just got the news today. I'll be in touch,' I answered in a nonchalant tone, trying to disguise how hurt I was. The clunking sound of that heavy handset landing on its receiver was followed by the thought that continued to be my mantra for many years: 'I'm all alone.'"

"What about your parents? Did you tell them?"

"Yes, a few days later. My mom had a new boyfriend now and they lived several hours away. I told her over the phone and her response was something like, 'Let me know what you decide.'"

"I told my father in person and the only thing I remember was him asking, 'How will you be able to finish school?' Both responses were made with good intentions and with concern for me. But neither took into account the new life inside of me. I was angry with both of them for many years, but we worked through it after I went through the healing program."

"How'd you finally decide?"

"I felt a tremendous amount of internal pressure to make my decision quickly. I needed this nightmare to be over. I reckoned there were three choices: adoption, becoming a parent, or abortion.

"Adoption was the first and the easiest to be rejected. *If I gave the baby to another, I'd have to think about it every year on its birthday. That would be too painful,* I decided.

"Becoming a parent was next on the list. I don't even remember considering the physical birthing part of the equation, probably because I wasn't thinking of my 'being pregnant' as 'having a baby inside of me'. I was simply focusing on the long-term commitment of parenting. I knew that other girls had gotten help from the fathers of their children, but that would require proving who it was. Back then there wasn't a kit you could buy in the pharmacy where you can mail off a piece of hair of the child and the potential father to prove paternity. I would have had to navigate the medical system, that to this point was suggesting abortion. It would require blood draws. I would have to tell both the potential fathers that they were not the only one. I lived in a small town and news traveled fast.

"And if I didn't finish college, I believed I'd be sentenced to poverty for the rest of my life. There must have been a part of me that desired to mother. Otherwise, I wouldn't have been abstaining from smoking and drinking during the time I was making my decision. *I'm barely able to support myself, how in the world could I support a child too?* I thought.

"Last on the list was abortion. *Now was the time to be practical*, I reasoned. Michelle had two abortions and said it was no big deal. I would be able to return to college. No one would have to know that I didn't know who the father was."

"Every rejection of the potential life inside of me felt like it was more support to the conclusion that I myself was of no value. And that was a feeling I wanted to be rid of. It appeared that abortion was the only solution that wouldn't affect me for the rest of my life.

"So with Helen Reddy's, 'I am woman, hear me roar' song playing in my head, I made another call to Ben. 'I have the money and made an appointment for the end of this week. You need to be here by Thursday at four,' he said.

"Do you know that song?"

"No," Meg replied.

"It's a song from the early '70s about women being strong and invincible and not needing help from anyone."

"Oh, got it. So Ben had already made the appointment?" asked Meg.

"Yes, and I took a seven-hour bus trip to his school. He met me just before the appointment, and we walked to the clinic which was just across the parking lot from the school dorms. I sat in the lobby filling out the forms, and I remember looking up to see Ben standing at the reception desk handing over the two hundred dollars. That was 47 years ago, and I can still pull the image up in my mind like it was yesterday."

Meg could see deep into the eyes of a scared, lonely young girl as Liz once again shared the hardest part.

"The counseling consisted of one question: 'Are you sure you want to do this?' My answer was 'Yes.' That one-word response carried with it all of the expectations I'd been led to believe were reasonable. Of course I wanted to have a simple, painless procedure with no side effects. One that would allow me to continue on with my life with no ramifications and be forgotten about in a few days, like a dental appointment.

"I was escorted down a long hallway and into a room. They inserted a laminaria stick inside of me to dilate my cervix, and I was told to return the next morning. That night was spent curled up on a dorm-room floor, crying from the pain, but doing it softly enough as to not wake the two young men sleeping on their beds. I'm pretty sure Ben offered me his bed but I didn't want to *need* anything from him.

"The only memories I carry with me of that next morning are of walking down that same hallway, going into a different room, climbing up on the table, having a long metal suction tube inserted inside of me, and the excruciating pain. I have no memories of leaving the clinic, the bus trip home, or three days of work.

"My memory returned Monday afternoon as I opened a notice from the clinic stating 'All of the tissue has successfully been removed.' At first I felt relief, thinking the nightmare was over. But really it'd just begun. I was fired from my daytime job for sleeping in and failing to open the deli on time, and I moved away from the hotel and into an apartment with a friend.

"My weekend partying quickly transitioned into a daily event. One morning, as I lit up a joint before eating breakfast, I thought to myself, 'This is what a pothead does. So now I'm a pothead, an all-alone pothead.'

"I reconnected with that friend many years later. She had so many memories of that year and I was unable to recall any of them. When I returned to school, I felt very different than the other students. My studies and work kept me busy, so I only smoked some evenings and most weekends, no longer during the day."

"What degree did you get?" asked Meg.

"I didn't graduate. Even though it was a fresh start for me, the excitement for my future was gone. I was lonely and cried a lot when no one was around but didn't understand why. Every once in a while I recognized that I was crying because I'd had an abortion, but considering that everything I'd read and heard about abortion sounded empowering, I just figured something was wrong with me, so I dismissed it.

At the end of that school year, I met Charles, the guy who I believed was to be my knight in shining armor."

"How did you meet him?" asked Meg.

"He was traveling around the east coast with friends of my roommates and they crashed at our house for the week. We stayed up all night talking the first night. We discovered that we both had parents who'd recently divorced after 21 years of marriage and that our mothers had both married alcoholics named Frank. We shared our dreams for the future. Both of us wanted lots of children and neither of us were active in faith or religion. We both were determined not to follow in our parent's path of divorce. We considered the couples we knew who seemed to have what we wanted and came to the conclusion that the common denominator in all of them was that they were Christian. A small seed was planted with that conversation."

"So was he your knight in shining armor?"

"He was and still is an amazing guy and I'm extremely blessed to be spending my life with him. However, there wasn't a single person on earth who could have given to me what I needed. Even in our first years together I would get extremely angry over little things. My instant response was either bottling up my feelings and shutting him out or screaming at the top of my lungs. There was little if any middle ground. I only smoked a few times after meeting Charles because he didn't like it. In fact we only smoked together one time. Because of this change, the memories from my past had more access to my mind. I started having recurring nightmares, flashbacks, anxiety attacks, and would try to find some control in my life by dieting or obsessive cleaning."

"But that all went away when you had children, right?" asked Meg.

"I'd assumed they would. As soon as I was pregnant again, I got my hands on every baby development book I could. When I read that at ten weeks the fingernails were developed, I thought *'that means they were almost developed when I....'* And the first time I felt the baby move, I thought, *'only three weeks after I...'* I had to push the thoughts out of my mind. I had to, the alternative was just too hard to face.

"It was confusing because *now* I had a husband and a home. *'I should be happy,'* I thought. But instead, as each pregnancy milestone was reached, it only seared into my heart an even greater awareness of the amazing miracle that had been discarded during that appointment. I remember just a few days after our first child's birth, Charles and I were lying on the living room floor with her tucked between us. We found joy in simply looking at Lee. We gazed at her fingers, toes, eyes, every part of her. To think that our passion for each other could produce such a miracle! I loved to hold, nurse, and care for her, but she didn't fill that gaping hole in my heart. She couldn't, and neither could the rest of our children.

"Carol was such a sweet little girl, but having two children I struggled to bond with just made me more exhausted. Shortly after her birth, Charles suggested we try to find a neighborhood church to plug into. We visited a few and then settled on a start-up Presbyterian church close to our home. We attended for several years, and although it was a good move for our social life, the church failed to promote the gospel message which I so dearly needed.

"I attended a Bible study for another church where the issue of abortion came up during a discussion of the Ten Commandments. We were on number six, 'Thou shall not murder', when someone brought up abortion. Someone else said something like, 'I can't believe any woman could be so selfish as to kill her own child.' I quickly left and didn't return, even after the host called and invited me back.

"Looking back I remember constantly feeling anxious. I know now that I was spinning my wheels with what I call 'if onlys'. If only the house were perfectly clean, the children were always happy and well dressed, I were the perfect weight, or if everyone thought I was the perfect mother. I saw a career as a critical necessity, since I needed to have a way to provide for myself and the children when Charles left. Because in *my* mind, the men always left. So as each child was born, the pressure to find a higher-paying job increased.

"Renee', our third child, was sick within weeks of being born. She suffered from continual infections and breathing problems and was rarely able to sleep unless being held upright on my chest. Just after her second birthday, we took her to a surgery clinic to have her tonsils and adenoids removed. Due to complications, she ended up being admitted to the children's hospital for what turned into a seven-day stay.

"A few months later, while caring for our three girls and two of their cousins for the week, I found myself unable to function. Grabbing the nearby telephone, I called our family doctor and said to the receptionist, 'I need help'. The prescribed remedy for my diagnosis of situational depression was antidepressants, which did little to solve the root problem. My anxiety was somewhat controlled, but the medicine really slowed me down. I depended on the busy-ness to keep me distracted, so I went off the medication within a few months."

Are you still doing okay, Meg?" Liz asked

"Yes, I really want you to keep going."

"Okay, I just need to let you know that the next part might be hard to hear, so please know that if it's too much, just say so and I'll stop. Okay?"

"Yes, okay," she agreed.

"That spring, Charles and I went to see a movie called 'The Joy Luck Club'. It's a story of four Chinese mothers and the personal and cultural clashes they have with their daughters who were raised in America. One of the mothers flashed back to a scene where she's at home bathing a little boy about three years old. She heard a fumbling at the door and found her husband drunk and trying to come in with another woman. She attempted to stop him but he forced his way in. Crying and in a trance-like state, she returned to the bathtub, grabbed her son by the shoulders, and proceeded to push him under the water, holding him there until his body stopped moving. My reaction to the scene was instant hatred for the woman. Then that hatred was turned inward as I asked myself, 'how are *you* any better?'.

"I held it together the best I could for the remainder of the movie but started crying on the drive home. When we arrived and Charles got out of the drivers seat, I quickly slipped in. He didn't want me to leave, but was reassured when I told him, 'Don't worry, I'll be alright. I just need to spend some time alone.'

"It was 11 years after my abortion, and I was driving down the streets of Cleveland, sobbing uncontrollably, terrified, and feeling as if I were separated from my body, unable to control it or anything it did. I found a hotel, checked into a room, and immediately fell to the floor letting out a loud guttural wail. The kind you might imagine when seeing a photo of a mother holding the lifeless body of her child at the scene of a bombing.

"I lay there on the floor crying until there was nothing left. Then I picked up a pen and paper and began writing. I wrote letters to my aborted child, my three daughters, Charles, my parents, and my brothers. I wrote until the sun came up. I knew I needed help. I knew my problems were related to my abortion, but I didn't know where to turn, or who to turn to. People were so divided on the issue of abortion. There didn't appear to be any middle ground.

"Remembering the comment made at the Bible study confirmed my fears that condemnation and judgment were at the core of the "pro-life" message. I reasoned that "pro-choice" people weren't interested in hearing that I was hurting from my abortion. I'd already heard and had even told myself statements that minimized the event. 'You did what was right for you at the time', 'You have children now right?', or 'Look how much better off you are than you would have been as a single mother.' Joining with them would simply require that I deny what my heart really knew. That I had lost a child and I needed to mourn my loss.

"I saw myself at a crossroads of sorts, with one path leading to condemnation and the other leading to justification."

"So I went home from that hotel room, stuffing my shredded heart back into a body that was only going through the motions, and returned to the game of pretending to be a wonderful mother. The mental break I'd experienced brought about an even greater need to be in control and though I wasn't aware of it at the time, I was terrified of becoming pregnant again without planning for it. I'd struggled with headaches from several different birth control methods over the years and now we'd settled on a natural 'family planning' method, abstaining during ovulation. We used it successfully for years, but now we were becoming less diligent about keeping track.

"Fall, my season of sadness, was approaching again, and in desperation I pressured Charles into getting a vasectomy. Two weeks after the procedure, I told my mom I was feeling nauseous and wasn't sure I should travel for Thanksgiving. She told me she noticed some blotchy marks on my face, telltale signs of past pregnancies. My fears were confirmed with a home pregnancy test.

"I was 32 years old when Newman arrived, and I did my best to continue the outward charade of a perfect family. Charles no longer shared with me how his work day went, no longer invited me to his work social functions, and got home from work later and later. *Why would he be doing any different?* I thought. In fact, part of me was angry because he could escape from me and I couldn't. My anger outbursts had grown to a near daily event, occurring anytime things didn't go my way. The only release I had came in the form of screaming at Charles and our two oldest children. I'd give anything to go back and do those years over."

"The next few years Charles made continual attempts to connect with me emotionally, but I'd built a fortress around my heart and no one was going to get through. We were both very lonely. Though neither of us was physically unfaithful, we did both become attracted to others. Fall came again as it always did and, no longer able to continue with the way things were, I decided to move back to where the rest of my family lived. I figured If I was going to be a single mother of four, I was going to need their help.

"Fortunately, Charles refused to give up on our marriage. I thank God he took his marriage vows more seriously than I had. I found a job in Pennsylvania, Charles quit his job in Cleveland, we rented out our house, and piled into the vehicles of the moving caravan. I remember the children had their recently collected buckets of Halloween candy to help them pass the time during the long trip. We'd succeeded in moving our seriously damaged marriage to another state, but of course that wasn't enough. We went to several marriage counselors, with little improvement. Abortion was never brought up in those sessions. Charles knew I'd had one: he just didn't understand its deep impact. And I still wasn't able to face it.

"Charles and I were still living in the same house, but our inability to connect emotionally only confirmed my fears of being abandoned, and it was looking like our marriage was over. I even went so far as to write a list of things I would look for in a man when I started dating again. So that's kind of a long answer to your question, but no – the problems didn't go away when I had another child."

Liz paused, looked straight into Meg's tear-filled eyes, and asked with a smile, "Are you ready for the *good* news now?"

"Oh, yes!" Meg replied with a sigh of relief.

"Charles and I were again looking for a church to attend. Some family friends invited us to one in our community that had great children's programs. As hesitant as I was to be around those I perceived as judgmental and condemning, I wanted something better for our children. I knew that God loved and wanted good things for His children. I'd just concluded that I wasn't nor could I ever be one of them. A few months later, I signed up for a women's rafting trip put on by the church. I wasn't looking for any deep spiritual connection, only for the chance to try out a new adventure. I was in for an adventure all right, but it had very little to do with rafting.

"The speaker shared how important it was to have friends who really *knew you,* would laugh with you, cry with you, and support you when you needed it. These friends not only needed to know your greatest joys, but your greatest sorrows as well. She added that in order to maintain these friendships, we needed to nurture them. Our homework that night was to write down a list of our five closest friends. Then we were to note some actions we could take in order to make those friendships stronger.

"Later that night, I sat down with my leather day planner, turning to the back where the blank sheets were stored. I was ready to write my list, but I couldn't think of a *single* name to write down. I looked around and noticed the other ladies writing fervently. 'How could that be?' I thought, 'My calendar is completely full. I'm managing a bank, taking children to school functions, and attending church.'

"Not only did I not have a single friend like the speaker described, but I'd been without one nearly my entire adult life. I looked around at the ladies surrounding me and felt a little glimmer of hope, thinking to myself, 'There are 40 women here; maybe *one* of them could be my friend.'"

"Two weeks later, during a church service, one of the women from the rafting trip made an announcement about an upcoming study. She shared, in front of nearly 500 people, that she'd had an abortion and had suffered until she went through a post-abortion Bible study offered by the local pregnancy resource center. She listed the things she'd struggled with and I could relate with most of them. She said, 'I've learned many people suffer but it's difficult to find help because they don't want anyone to know they had one. It can be scary to face, but you don't have to face it alone. You'll make some friends along the way, and we'll be there to help you.'

"I couldn't believe it, and was thinking to myself, 'Had she just said the *abortion* word in church? In front of all these people?' That little glimmer of hope I'd recently experienced was enough to spur me on. I found her after the service and told her I needed to join the study. The truth is, I figured I had nothing to lose at this point. It was like another crossroads for me. I'd spent the last 17 years suffering, running on a treadmill and constantly looking for something or someone else to blame for my lack of peace.

"For 12 weeks, four other women and I were gently led through what turned out to be the most difficult yet most important journey of my life. This was not some magic study that solved all my problems overnight, but rather the beginning of a new life for me. My heart ached as others shared their stories, and I experienced a newfound freedom when the weight of long-held burdens fell away while sharing mine.

"We learned that although we played a big part in our abortion decisions, there were other people and factors that influenced us. We learned how much God loved us and how it was untrue that we could never be forgiven. We became aware of the running dialogue going on in our minds and its effect on our self-esteem, and we learned constructive ways to express our anger. With our leader's help, we uncovered long-held destructive patterns that were keeping us from experiencing love, joy, and peace.

"I learned that the reason I had no friends was because I was rejecting them first, to spare myself the future pain of them rejecting me. And I realized that I too was worthy of being loved, which enabled me to start the long process of rebuilding the many broken relationships in my life. I let go of my expectations of Charles to save me, my children to replace the one I'd lost, and my parents to protect the little girl I no longer was. It took years to repair our marriage but was worth every tear and heartache along the way."

"I now saw Charles not as the knight in shining armor that let me down, but as my best friend who'd refused to give up even when most would have. I was now able to accept the purest form of love here on earth, which was from our children. The two oldest had been emotionally abandoned so it took years before they could trust me again, but it was most definitely worth the effort it took to get there. Now I could look back on my poor choices and their ramifications with regret, rather than the shame and self-hatred that had been my constant companions.

"We learned that 43% of women in the U.S. had experienced one or more abortions, and I was filled with a passion to help them. I was one of the lucky few who'd found healing, and out of gratefulness for my new life, I had a mission. And since then, I've been open with my story and so here I am sharing with you."

"So you don't have any of those problems anymore?" asked Meg.

"After going through the study, most were gone completely and some showed up occasionally for several years, but with less intensity. As the gap between the occurrences widened, I became better at recognizing them for what they were and learned to dismiss them. The only thing that's continued and I believe will for the rest of my life is the nightmares. Only they've been different since my healing."

"How're they different?"

"Well, it used to be that I'd hear a baby crying, and I'd search but could never find it. After the study and as I began to help others, the dreams changed to trying to help others who are drowning or in burning buildings. In a sense the dreams are like reality in that I'm not able to help everyone. It's a hard thing to bear. However, if I let that discourage me and fail to continue on, then *none* will be helped. When I meet with people considering abortion, and they end up going through with it, they know right away where to turn if they start having problems. Hopefully they won't have to suffer as long as I did."

"I have the same dream every night," whispered Meg in a barely audible tone.

"If you'd like to tell me about it, I'm here to listen. Often it's the things we *can't* talk about that end up controlling us."

Meg

"I hear a crying baby- in different places, but most often around the high school. No one else can hear it except me. I run towards the sound which gets louder as I get closer." Meg continued at an increasing pace, her eyes shut tightly. "The baby's screaming at full pitch by the time I get to where it is, but it's always covered by something- a big pile of clothes, or books, or boxes of food. As I move those things out of the way, the crying gets softer. I'm sure the baby's still there and the pile's getting smaller, so I'm hopeful that I'll find it.

"But as I get to the bottom the crying fades away completely and I am left with nothing. My arms are always empty. Then I wake up and remember what I did. I'm scared to fall back asleep because the dream might return. But I need to because I'm just so tired of being exhausted."

"Oh, Meg," responded Liz gently. "I'm so sorry you're suffering, and I'm hoping you'll trust me enough to continue."

"I already do," Meg admitted with a reserved smile. "I really *want* to tell you more, but it's hard to get my mind around it. I really don't know where to start."

"Would it make it easier if I just asked you questions?"

"Yes, I think that would be easier, thank you."

"Okay then, what can you tell me about the father?"

"I met Toby the start of my junior year. I was a TA in one of his classes and the teacher asked me to help him so he'd get into the school he had a football scholarship from. He was a wrestler, too, but his real love was football."

"Toby asked me to the homecoming dance, and, before it was over, asked me to the Christmas dance as well. He was the first boy I dated. We agreed not to have sex right away, 'cause it would just complicate things. We both agreed to talk about it again over the summer.

"His friends were cool and super fun to hang with. Sometimes we'd drink a beer or two but that was all. We always had a designated driver because none of us wanted to mess up our college plans by getting in trouble.

"A few weeks before the Christmas dance, Toby started hanging out with a new guy on the wrestling team. Chip was a junior who moved here from California and had lots of money, I think his dad's some sort of wine importer. He didn't like hanging out with our group. A couple of times, when Toby said he was busy, I later found out he was out with Chip.

"I was stoked about the Christmas dance 'cause I was on the court. We doubled with one of the other wrestlers. His parents made us a steak dinner and we ate by candlelight. The dance was awesome, too. I wasn't crowned queen but never planned on it- everyone knows it's always the senior who wins.

"Chip was at the dance, too, and it was almost over when he asked Toby if he'd share me for just one song. I remember feeling funny when he got close to me, but didn't know why.

"After the dance, Toby said he needed to stop by Chip's place, then we'd head over to our favorite restaurant to meet up with the rest of our friends. I stayed in the car while Toby ran in. The house was huge, at least twice as big as most of our friends' houses, and Chip had an entire apartment all to himself. When Toby got back in the car, he had some gummy candies with him. He popped two in his mouth and handed the last three to me, which of course I ate.

"We both wanted to be alone together, so we didn't stay long at the restaurant. It seemed like only minutes later we were down by the river making out. Only this time, we sped right past the point where Toby had always stopped. It felt like I'd been swept up into all kinds of feelings I'd never had before and I didn't want them to stop. The next morning I realized we'd taken a chance, but I decided there was nothing I could do about it now. I just knew I was going to be smarter next time.

"During Christmas break, a friend told me she'd heard Chip bragging about introducing Toby to the joys of some 'special' candy. He was on a wrestling trip, but I texted him anyway. 'Anything unusual about those candies we ate after the dance?' His smart ass answer was, 'Well, I'd say so; *you* sure seemed to enjoy them, didn't you?' I was so pissed off. We'd just put our futures at risk and he was joking about it. Now I understood why my usual guard had come down. We'd agreed not to have sex. I wasn't on birth control, and he certainly didn't seem concerned enough to wear protection. He'd be back in three more days, and things were going to be different going forward.

"I was surprised when I heard he was back in town the very next day. He told me he'd come home early because he decided he didn't want to wrestle anymore. He seemed so angry with himself, said something about needing to get back on track. We made plans to get together that night. What I had to tell him needed to be said in person.

"It was all over Facebook that afternoon. He and Chip were kicked off the team and sent home after being caught selling THC-laced candy to kids from another school. They were both on probation, expelled from school, and he might lose his scholarship. I was ready to move on. Thank God for caller ID. I just ignored all his calls. I was ready for a fresh start without him. Only things weren't quite so simple.

"A couple of weeks later I realized my period was late. I told my sister. She immediately whipped out a pregnancy test from her purse. Sure enough, I was pregnant. She told me not to stress about it, she could help me, and no one else needed to know. My mind was racing and I wanted to turn the clock back just a few weeks.

"I answered a call from Toby that afternoon, and agreed to meet him at a coffee shop. He asked me to please just listen to him for a bit, and I agreed. He seemed like the Toby I used to know, and he apologized for so many things. For letting Chip influence him, for dragging me into it, for allowing what happened to happen. He said he wasn't going back to high school, was getting his GED, and planned to enroll in the local community college. He was going to get two years under his belt, then transfer to a state university. His parents had agreed to pay for all his expenses through college as long he stayed out of trouble.

"He grabbed my hand and said that what he wanted more than anything was for me to give him another chance, so he could prove that he was worth hanging in there with.

"When I told him I was pregnant, I expected him to pull his hand away, but instead he was silent for a moment.

'Well, that's all the more reason why you need to give me another chance', he said.

"He told me he wanted to do the right thing, and we could make it work. He'd get a job while going to school. He said he was sure his parents would still pay for his school and after he finished, I could go to school.

"It all sounded like a challenge, but still possible. I was on track for an early graduation. If I took summer classes, I could be finished before the baby was born. Then it would only be three years until Toby finished college. We could take out loans for me, since he'd have a good job.

"He wanted to wait a while before telling his parents. He first wanted to show them how serious he was about getting started at the college. Also, by then they'd see that he'd hold up his promise to stay clean. I told Wendy about our plans and she was less than thrilled."

"What did she say?" Liz asked.

"She said, 'There go our plans to start a law practice together. It all sounds like a fairytale now, but just wait. You won't make it back to school. You probably won't even stay together. There's still time to change your mind. *Do not* tell mom and dad unless you have to.'

"I wanted so much to believe my sister was wrong, so I reasoned she was just jealous of my plans. Fortunately it was winter, which made it easy to hide my changing body. Big, heavy sweaters and lots of layers can do wonders.

"January flew by and I started imagining being a mom. Toby and I talked about baby names and held our secret close. Only he and I and Wendy knew.

"Mid-term grade reports were due out the start of March, and our plan was to tell our parents then. Toby had all A's so far, he'd passed every one of his drug tests, and only hung out with me and one of his old high school friends, the one we went to the dance with.

"Spring was just around the corner and I was looking forward to switching over to some cooler shirts, just as soon as the news was out. We'd been together nearly every day and then he came down with the flu. We didn't want to take any chances of me catching it from him and I missed him terribly for several days. I'd offered to pick up and drop off some of his homework, but he said his mom had already taken care of it.

"Finally Toby called and asked me to meet him for coffee. The moment he walked in, I knew something was different. He wouldn't look me in the eye, he didn't hug me before sitting down and he was fidgeting. 'Our plans have changed,' he said coolly. 'My parents are *not* on board with our plans. They say if we go through with this that I need to move out this month, and I can forget about them paying for college. My dad said he's seen too many lives ruined and he's not about to subsidize our plans. He said that when I graduate from college, I'll get $25,000 from my Grandma. They'll pay for the abortion and counseling for you if you want it.'

"'Wow,' was all I could say. My heart felt like it was beating out of my chest. I was in shock. He just looked at me, his jaw tight and his arms crossed. 'Meg, $25,000 is a lot of money! You'll almost have your bachelor's degree by then. We could get married and have kids then; just think about it.' he said.

"It was warm that day and driving home I had to turn on the air conditioning. The bulky sweater I had on was suffocating me. I went right to my room, closed the door, and sobbed for hours. Wendy was over for dinner and as usual she ignored my wishes to be left alone. After I told her the news, she hugged me and said, 'I'm so glad you haven't told mom and dad. It makes things much easier. This is really a good thing for you, and it'll be over in a few days. You don't need this guy anyway, and you certainly don't need his parents' money. I'll pay for it. I have so many friends who've had abortions, and you're far enough along that they'll put you completely out.'

"Before I could say anything, Wendy was on her phone making an appointment. We look so much alike, that she used all her own information- her age, her home address- everything possible to hide what was being set up.

"I was scheduled for Saturday morning. We told our parents we were spending the day shopping and celebrating my upcoming birthday. Wendy would pick me up at 10. Toby ignored all my texts over the next few days. It was clear he wasn't there for me, unless I followed through.

"Part of me was hoping he'd have a change of heart, but it didn't look like that was going to happen. I sent him my last text Friday night, 'My appointment is tomorrow. I don't need you and I don't need your money. You're an asshole.'"

"But this text *did* get a response, only it wasn't from Toby. It was from his friend. He said he saw my text and Toby had just told him what was going on. He said he was adopted and knew some people who could help. He was begging me not to go through with it. 'Too late, thanks though,' was all I texted back. Then I turned off my phone."

"I laid out my heavy sweater for the next morning. My last thought before falling asleep was, 'I'm never wearing that again.' The next morning Wendy filled out the paperwork and paid the money while I sat in the lobby. No one was talking, and all of us there, including a few guys, were looking at the floor."

Meg, clutching a pillow tight against her belly, had tears streaming down her face and was rocking back and forth as she continued. "I signed a piece of paper with lots of writing on it that I didn't read. The woman behind a desk asked me a couple of questions that I don't remember answering. It pretty much seemed like I was watching a movie. The last thing I remember is the mean-looking nurse putting the mask over my face.

"Then I heard my mom's voice from the hallway. I was home in bed. My pillows were flung all over the room and my head felt as if it were ready to explode. I didn't remember coming home.

"She wanted to know if I was going hiking with her and dad. I lied and told her I had too much homework. The truth was, I *did* have a lot of homework but couldn't care less whether it got done. I saw my sweater lying at the end of the bed. A loose strand of yarn was sticking out and I reached down to pull it. The loops and stitches came apart easily and I felt powerful destroying something that had tortured me for so long. The rows dissolved easily and the loose yarn pile grew higher than what was left of the sweater. It pissed me off when the whole thing stopped because of a knot. I threw my blankets off so I could grab the pair of scissors on my desk.

"I freaked out when I saw blood all over my thighs and the bed. Wendy had told me it should be pretty much like a regular period, and this was way more than that. I stood up quickly and almost passed out. It took awhile to get my balance. I was terrified my mom would come to the door again, so I quickly pulled off the blankets and sheets and stuffed them under the bed.

"All I wanted was to get into the shower. I grabbed my bathrobe, shoved the rest of my sweater between my legs, and headed down the hall. Once I got inside the bathroom and locked the door, I couldn't wait to get clean. The hot water felt wonderful and after awhile, the water at my feet changed from dark red to light pink and then to clear.

"I saw some mold on the tile and reached out under the sink to get the scrub brush. But as soon as that spot was gone, I noticed others and it seemed as if the more I scrubbed, the more mold showed up. Now I was scrubbing frantically- both the tile and then myself - but I still felt dirty. I sprinkled the rough cleaner all over me and ground it into my skin with a washcloth. Now the water was turning cold, very cold, and when I became numb, somehow the dirty feeling went away.

"My parents had left by the time I made it out to the kitchen. Mom had left homemade biscuits and strawberry freezer jam- my favorite breakfast- but today the smell turned my stomach. I didn't want food. I needed another shower.

"I took at least six of them that day. I discovered that rather than going through the slow process of running out of hot water, I could just start with the cold. The numbness came quicker that way.

"The next morning, the last thing I wanted to do was go to school. I couldn't imagine sitting in the cafeteria listening to my friends, concerned about taking the SAT, and what color they were going to paint their nails. And then there were the two classes I had with Jordan, Toby's friend who tried to help me."

Meg was too engrossed in her story to notice Liz's expression as she made the connection.

"I lied to my mom again and told her I was staying home because I had the flu. I couldn't get into the shower fast enough. After the third one, I realized I needed to find another way of getting through the day. I thought about Chip. I knew he was back at school and wondered if he really was clean or if maybe he could hook me up with something, maybe some more of those candies. Turning on my phone to call him, I saw that I had two messages.

"The first was from Toby. He pretended to care but really just wanted to know if 'things were taken care of'. The next was from Jordan. He said he was worried about me, that I might be confused and hurting. He said he knew a lady that helps girls like me and that she'd meet with me whenever I was ready.

"I still had some Christmas money, and Chip was more than happy to deliver the first bag of candy. I knew right away this was the answer to my problems. It helped me forget how dirty I felt, it gave me an appetite, and just helped me not care anymore.

"Returning to school the next day wasn't as bad as I feared. I saw Jordan in the hallway but turned my head the other way as we passed. The lacrosse coach looked confused when I told her not to plan on me joining this year. Chip found me at my locker right after lunch. I knew by the way he hugged me that if I was willing to give him what he wanted, he'd keep me supplied with what I needed.

"All in all, it was okay for the rest of the school year, except that my grades tanked. I found a waitress job over the summer. We were all wasted most of the day, so it was easy. Chip worked there, too. His dad travels a lot, so I spent a lot of time at his place.

"I never returned Toby's text, and he never tried to reach me again. Last I heard, he's off at a four-year college and has a new girlfriend.

"Just before school started this year, Chip told me he was moving. It felt like I was nothing more than a customer he had to inform. I started crying, not because I cared about him- I didn't- but because I was losing my supply. The money I earned over the summer was already set aside for college, in a joint account with my mom. She'd know if I pulled it out. My parents weren't giving me allowance anymore because my grades were so bad. I could keep working during school, but I didn't have a way to get there. I'd lost my license after getting a DUI. My parents wouldn't let me drive their car anyway because of my bad grades.

"I found some of my dad's leftover Vicodin in the medicine cabinet. It helped with my anxiety, but it made it hard to read or focus on anything at school.

"It's been hard to be around my parents since my abortion. They keep trying to help me, but I can't tell them what I did. I don't want to hurt them, but just seeing what's happening to me is hurting them.

"My sister's always yelling at me, saying things that are true and that I deserve to hear. In fact, she was yelling at me right before the accident. I'd tried to kill myself by overdosing and she was worried. And as if things weren't bad enough already, Jordan got hurt really bad saving the woman in the car we hit.

"I haven't cared about anything for so long, and up until recently, I didn't have any hope things were going to change."

"What happened that gave you hope?" asked Liz

"Jorie told me her plan for getting me off drugs and back on track for graduating. And now meeting you, I feel like I can trust you guys."

"Meg, you *can* trust us. And I can't help but feel that, as hard as it's been, you're going to be okay. Did you know I've known Jordan all his life?"

"No way. Really?" asked Meg, not even trying to hide her astonishment.

"He's like a grandson to my husband and me, and he's been living with us since his freshman year. In fact, it was our house you came to before the Christmas dance last year. His parents fixed the meal. Jordan's the reason I came to the hospital today."

"Oh...." stammered Meg.

Liz was quiet for a bit, giving Meg a moment to think.

The texts from Jordan, the conversation with Karina. Meg's mind raced. *Now she knows I'm the reason Jordan might die. I was foolish to trust her, she has good reason to hate me. Looks like once again, I'm getting what I deserve.*

"Meg," Liz said softly. "Thank you so much for sharing your story. I know it's not easy, but it's really important. We have another healing program starting up in a few weeks. Would you like to join us?"

"Do I have to tell my parents about it?" asked Meg.

"No, and I'm so glad you asked because it's important you know that your participation is extremely confidential. If you tell anyone, it'll be on your terms. You'll be required to have two support people during the program, but we have many women willing to be that for you. Many of them have made the same choice you did and have already been through the program."

Meg couldn't believe Liz still cared about her even after she found out she was the reason Jordan was injured.

Feeling scared, yet like she had nothing to lose, Meg replied, "I'd like to join."

"Awesome! Hopefully we can visit again before then. How long do you think you'll be in here?"

"I'll be out of *here* before the end of next week," Meg answered with just a hint of confidence. "But the therapy I'll be coming back for will last months."

"Okay, I'll leave one of my cards for you at the reception desk. They made me leave my backpack there," Liz said. "I'll be visiting Jordan several times a week. Perhaps you can join me in his room sometime?"

"Thank you, I'd like that." Though emotionally exhausted, Meg continued to process their conversation long after her new friend's departure. It seemed like Liz understood her in a way that even she didn't.

As the tears poured out, she felt the empty space left behind being replaced with hope. She knew that no matter how impossible it seemed that she could be freed from the pain, she *had* to try. She couldn't continue this way. The only other option was death, and apparently she couldn't even get *that* right. That night, for the first time in months, deep restful sleep came easy.

When Meg opened her eyes the next morning, she smiled to herself as the pillows still surrounding her came into focus. *Could this be the same room I've been in since Friday?* she asked herself. It was as if she were seeing it for the first time. Instead of delivering pain, the bright winter sunlight streaming through the window caressed her gently.

Even the food delivered later on a large plastic tray seemed different. There was still a lot of room for improvement, but now she saw it as fuel for her body rather than something she *had* to consume in order to appease others. Halfway through the meal, she was surprised by a tinge of longing for her mom's biscuits and strawberry freezer jam. Her surroundings seemed less like a cage and more like a temporary place to rest before embarking on a really big journey.

"Hey, Meg. How are you feeling today?" Jorie asked, entering the room a few hours later. She was delighted to see Meg writing in a journal.

"Very good, thanks. I slept so well. I think maybe I'd forgotten what it feels like to be rested," replied Meg.

"Awesome, that's great to hear. Hopefully you'll have many more nights like that. What do you attribute the change to?"

"Well, I'm not really sure how to explain it. Liz came to visit me yesterday and I'm gonna be in the next healing program. She really seems to understand me and I'm thinking that program might help. Also, my brain just feels clear again, so maybe the detox is helping too."

"Wonderful! I think you're feeling some hope about your future. Even your body language tells me you're feeling more positive. It literally shows on your face! I'm excited for you and I'm so proud of you for choosing to be honest and willing to do the work in your treatment program."

"I just wish I'd been feeling more hopeful last year. I used to be brave and strong."

"Meg, you still are brave *and* strong, you've just had a setback. You'll understand more when you're older and can look back on the awesome ways you've contributed to the world and those around you. It's often the roughest times in our lives that put us in the position to help others. Right now, you're only able to see your most recent trauma and your current situation, but that's improving, right?"

"Yeah, you're right," Meg acknowledged. "My sister, Wendy, is coming to visit me today. I want to tell her about my treatment plan. I'm also gonna ask her to join in on some of the group sessions."

"How about your parents? Do you think you may be open to talking with them now?"

"Talking with them yes, but I don't want them coming while I'm in here. It was prolly' hard enough seeing me in the ER, I think seeing me in here would be even worse."

"Sounds fair," Jorie conceded. "It sounds like you're on the right track. I think we need to start planning your transition out of here and on to your very bright future."

5. THE LONG HAUL

Karina

Although Karina loved spending weekends at home, catching up with family and close friends, being there was always overshadowed by the feeling that she needed to be at the hospital with Jordan. She was hoping to finish opening the previous week's worth of mail before heading back.

The steady flow of get well cards for Jordan had tapered off and she was taken aback by the sight of the first Christmas card. *Could it be that five weeks have passed since Jordan's accident?* she wondered.

Karina felt thankful for everyone who continued to visit him. In fact, she realized that between Meg, Liz, Trevor, his siblings, extended family, and friends, he'd seldom been alone.

It was just before nine the next morning when she stepped into Jordan's room, stopping as she noticed Meg was already there, even though it wasn't one of her therapy days. Karina made note of the changes in the young woman who appeared to be more comfortable with herself than she was before. Her hair, thick and shiny, was pulled loosely up into a soft ponytail, exposing bright eyes and filled-in cheeks that had color and lifted up every time she smiled.

Setting aside her schoolbooks, Meg picked up the guitar and started strumming. With eyes closed she leaned back against the wall, humming the most beautiful melody Karina had ever heard. She appeared to be giving full expression to deeply buried emotions- first heartache and despair, then hope, followed by celebration.

Karina stood frozen, not wanting to intrude, yet not wanting to miss a moment of it either. As the song came to an end, she scanned the room hoping to lock the memory of it in her mind forever.

The lattes cradled in Karina's hands nearly met an early fate when, glancing at Jordan, she saw the fingers on his right hand moving in a jerky attempt to keep time with the song. A shout of delight erupted from Karina, startling Meg and bringing the magical scene to a screeching halt.

Meg, frightened and embarrassed, jerked forward and shouted, "What? What is it?"

"He... he was moving his fingers!"

Just then Liz walked in. "It's snowing!" she announced with a smile. "Oh, I'm sorry if I've interrupted," she stammered when she realized both women were crying.

"No, Liz, it's a really *good* thing! Jordan moved his fingers!" shouted Karina.

The sounds of celebration echoed down the hallway, catching the attention of Heather, walking slowly on her way to visit Karina.

"What the heck's going on in here?" she asked, entering the room.

As Heather learned the wonderful news, she and Karina decided to stay in Jordan's room for their visit. Neither of them wanted to miss out on the excitement.

Introductions were made, and Liz was thrilled to meet the woman Jordan had saved. Meg was both relieved and grateful that Karina introduced her simply as one of Jordan's classmates.

Doctors and staff came and went, taking vital signs and testing Jordan's response to stimuli. The mood in the room was infectious to anyone who entered. Several attempts were made to re-create the scenario that brought about his response. Others played the guitar and sang, and although there was *some* movement, it paled in comparison to what Karina witnessed during Meg's melody.

Meg, though not willing to sing with others in the room, *was* willing to continue strumming it. Jordan showed a clear preference for her music over everyone else's, not only through his fingers, but now his toes as well.

Heather

"So Heather, how much longer 'til your delivery?" Liz asked after the medical staff cleared out.

"I'm at 30 weeks right now, and the doctor just told me this morning that they wouldn't stop it if labor started, but he'd prefer that I make it at least one more week. We want to give her every advantage possible and hopefully avoid any time in NICU."

"Oh, absolutely. It's obvious she's well loved. I'm so happy for you. Does she have a name?" inquired Liz.

"Not yet. We've got several in mind but seem to have trouble settling on one. We've lost three babies in the past, and I think I won't truly believe it until she's in my arms. Maybe then we'll name her."

"Names are so important, even for the ones that are lost. In fact, we built a memorial garden just for that purpose."

"So you have a child memorialized there?" asked Heather.

"Yes, I chose the name Adam for the child I lost to abortion. I found healing after suffering for 17 years, and ever since then have been sharing my story in hopes that others who need it will do the same."

Noticing that Heather appeared interested in hearing more, Liz offered to show her a short video of one of her speeches many years ago.

Heather felt conflicted as she watched. She'd always thought that women who chose abortion were selfish and unloving, very much unlike the one in front of her. It was hard to imagine that people would send Liz hate mail, scream at her in public, and treat her rudely when she shared her very personal story.

A few years back, Heather had read something about women suffering after their choice of abortion. She realized now that she'd been holding the stance that if anyone did suffer, they deserved it. After all, they were throwing away something she'd had taken from her time and time again and would have given anything to keep.

"So what other venues have you shared at?" she asked.

"Oh, let's see. Churches, pregnancy resource center banquets, youth groups, college pro-life group meetings, right to life meetings, radio, tv, civic organization meetings, and my favorites are classrooms and women's retreats."

Heather adjusted herself in the chair before asking, "Why are the last two your favorite?"

"I love middle and high school classrooms because of the greater potential for preventing abortions. I always leave room at the end for questions. Back before texting existed, I'd have them write their questions anonymously on a piece of paper they'd pass forward. Texting makes things easier.

"The most common question is how I feel about abortion in the case of rape or incest. My response is that, I don't judge anyone who chooses abortion. My heart breaks for them, and it's not my place to judge. However, I happen to know a young man who is the product of both rape and incest. When he hears statements like, "except in the case of rape or incest", he feels that others think he doesn't deserve to be alive. And I've read many affidavits from women who felt just as violated if not more so from their abortions than they did from being raped. Many felt that the abortion did little to help them forget their attack. You seldom hear them sharing this publicly due to the political and moral divide that permeates the issue.

"I'm often asked, 'Why didn't you research?' I then ask them 'how would *you* research if you or a close friend became pregnant?' The answer is usually, 'I'd go to the internet.' Then I usually say, 'Well, I'm not justifying my choice in 1981, but the internet was still eight years away from being invented. Other things that didn't exist were pregnancy resource centers, *Time Life Magazine* covers showing the stages of life in the womb, and people who speak out about the physical and emotional trauma they've experienced. But I do need to add that, even now with all these new things I've mentioned, people are still being deceived about its potential impact.

"I've had students and adults imply that the problems I've suffered from were all directly related to the guilt placed upon me by my religion. This is one of my favorite ones to dismantle with, 'It might be easy for you to conclude that, but first of all, it has nothing to do with *religion*. It's my *faith* that changed me. And the truth is, I didn't come into that *faith* until my healing program. And it was this *faith* that ended the 17 years of suffering.'"

"Ah, good point," agreed Heather.

"And the reason I love sharing at women's retreats is they usually last for three days, which gives ample time for connecting. I usually share on the first evening, giving out my cell phone number. It's very common for calls to start arriving by mid-Saturday. I'll meet privately with them, and it's not always because they've had an abortion. Since I've metaphorically exposed my underbelly by sharing such a personal story, they feel safe sharing their deep hurts and things they feel ashamed about. I love encouraging them and pointing towards resources that can help."

Heather made a quick personal commitment to be more conscious of the comments she made about abortion and those who choose it.

"You know, if it weren't for Liz finding healing and reaching out to help others, we would've never learned about Jordan's birth mom and the support she needed. The fact that he's alive is truly a miracle," Karina interjected.

"Well, I can honestly say I'm glad you found healing Liz- not only for yourself, but for us too," Heather added while patting her stomach. "The accident had such huge impacts on myself and especially Jordan, now I only wish I knew more about the young lady injured in the accident."

Karina quickly responded. "I've heard she's doing quite well. Perhaps you'll meet her one of these days, when she's ready. I'd imagine it'd be difficult for her, since she might feel responsible for what happened to both you and Jordan."

"Well, I'm sure neither she nor her sister *intended* for our cars to collide or for anyone to be hurt. I hope I get the chance to tell her I'm not holding any blame."

"I *did* want to hurt someone that day, but it wasn't you or Jordan. It was myself," whispered Meg apprehensively. "That feeling's gone now, and I just want to say I'm sorry and I really hope your little girl will be alright."

Heather paused, smiled at Liz, and looked back to Meg. "Apology accepted. It's nice to understand it all. Did you know Jordan before the accident?"

"Yes and no," replied Meg. "He tried to help me when my life was falling apart, but I didn't let him. It's good to be here now, but I sure hope to get the chance to talk with him and actually thank him."

"Yes, I'd love the chance to thank him as well," agreed Heather. "So which one of you ladies is going to fill me in on the life story of my hero lying over here?"

Heather and Meg listened intently as the story unfolded.

"The call came on a Sunday evening in April from one of the ladies in the healing program I lead," began Liz. "She told me she'd had a chance to pray for a young woman who'd visited her church that morning. 'Eva has an abortion scheduled for tomorrow, and she doesn't want to get it, will you meet with her?' she asked.

"Eva's hands trembled as she consumed one cigarette after another, ignoring the *no smoking* sign on a nearby wall in the tiny motel room. Her incomplete sentences tumbled out revealing her entire life story."

"Eva told me her mom was a prostitute in New York and she knew nothing about her father. She was handed over to an aunt shortly after birth and placed in foster care within a year. She suffered abuse in several foster homes before being adopted at eight."

"The diagnoses of mental illness came at age 13 but was kept under control with medication and supervision. She married at 19, and after a volatile four years found herself alone and living on the streets of Cleveland."

Liz continued, "The baby's father, another homeless person, held her captive for three months and was currently in jail because of it. The police had delivered her to a women's shelter in Wadsworth, Ohio, where Charles and I lived. She wasn't allowed to stay in the shelter because the other women were frightened of her. A government agency had her set up in a motel and had made several abortion appointments for her in Cleveland. She'd missed her ride for the first, changed her mind during the second, and had the third appointment scheduled for the next morning.

"Her body language became increasingly agitated and jerky as she vanished into her story. This appeared to be a perfect storm for the defense of abortion: mental illness, rape, *and* abuse.

"The fear of being in way over my head inundated my senses and I felt the urge to flee. Being cognizant that there was a life at stake was the only thing that kept me from doing so. I counted four steps to the door out of the hotel room and reasoned that since I had a few pounds on her, I'd stand a chance in a scuffle. Noting there were no weapons in sight, I decided to stay. I sent a quick text informing my husband of my location. Charles had grown accustomed to the many different facets of this ministry and understood *these* opportunities could never be scheduled.

"I entered into a dialogue with my only source of refuge at a time such as this. It wasn't audible, but more of a sensation within me.

'Lord, is there ever a time when abortion is okay? Because *if* there is, it seems like this might be it.'

'*How do you think the baby would answer?*' I sensed.

'*Okay, Lord, then what's my part?*'

'*To love her.*'

"'*That's not going to be easy*', I thought, returning my attention to Eva. But God had proven faithful during big challenges in the past so I chose to trust him once again.

"She was still sitting on the bed chain smoking when her monologue came to a close. I told her I wanted to help.

'Everyone says that, then after a while they give up. You will too,' she retorted.

"I told her I hoped to prove her wrong, then went on to share my story of suffering after having an abortion. I didn't want her to struggle the way myself and many others did.

"She was concerned that this was her only chance to get a ride to the clinic, so I promised to give her one if she changed her mind. Glancing at my phone, I was shocked to see that it was after two a.m.

"I told her I'd be back just before the taxi was expected and if she wanted, she could join me for breakfast."

"Pulling up to the motel a few hours later, I marveled at the notion that a life was on the line that very moment. She bounded out of the motel room, slid into the car, and seemed more excited about going out to eat than she did about her decision. We went out for breakfast and noticed a beautiful rainbow directly over the place we were headed next, the local pregnancy resource center.

"Eva had trouble concentrating as she heard about the free services available. If she parented, there were parenting classes to earn baby supplies and furniture. If she chose to adopt, she'd receive information about several agencies, and if she chose abortion and struggled later, there were programs to help with healing. She was shown development photos of babies in the womb and learned hers was about an inch and a half long, and had all their parts, including finger-and toenails. The most important thing she learned is that she wasn't alone. The people at the center would be there for her no matter what she decided.

"I had no idea how challenging my assigned task of *loving her* was going to be. But as I look back on the remainder of Eva's pregnancy, I can see God's fingerprints all over. I love that He provided everything and everyone in His perfect timing. From that day forward, she received housing, food, clothing, rides, and most importantly love. She was sheltered from the agencies which continued to push for the abortion until nearly the end of the summer."

"She told them she didn't want one, right?" Heather asked.

Meg, now listening, gasped as Liz replied, "Yep."

"And they continued to pressure her?" asked Heather.

"Oh yes, many times." Liz continued, "She asked me to come with her to all her appointments. I was pretty naive going into the first one. The lobby was packed by the time her number was called and the clerk impatiently asked if she'd gone to see the specialist. Eva looked at me, confused.

'He wants to know if you got the abortion,' I told her. 'Oh no, I'm not going to get an abortion,' she replied in a voice loud enough for everyone to hear.

'This is Liz, she had one and regrets it. She's going to help me.'

"He leaned forward to peer at me, then returned his gaze to Eva as if he needed reassurance that she was serious. Realizing she was, he shook his head in disbelief and began typing indignantly. Obviously I wasn't a welcome addition.

"A few days after one of her sessions, I got a call from her counselor.

'It appears Eva trusts you quite a bit,' he said.

'Yes, she does.' I answered.

'Though I commend you for trying, her case is simply one of those that falls through the cracks. I know it's frustrating but that's just the way it is. You're not going to be able to help her,' he stated with confidence.

'That may be the case, but I still have to try,' I rebutted.

"He then brought it up a notch with, 'She's been working for a pimp in Cleveland, and if he got word you're helping her, your family could be in danger. And your involvement could have legal repercussions as well.'

"'I appreciate your concern, but I still need to try,' I maintained.

"His intent became crystal clear when he emphatically blurted out, 'Liz, you need to set aside your philosophical and moral beliefs and do what's right. You need to convince

Eva to go through with the treatment plan. I need to hospitalize her, and the medicine she needs would be harmful for the baby.'

"A rush of adrenaline overpowered my ability to remain calm and I retorted sarcastically, 'Well, last time I checked, abortion wouldn't be too good for the baby either.'

"I can't remember his response, but after hanging up I thought to myself, *I didn't track down this woman, tie her up and tell her, 'You are not getting an abortion!' She found me through an amazing set of circumstances, asking for help. Yes, she trusted me, was that a bad thing? She trusted me because I didn't lie to her.*

"It seemed that I had no choice but to help her. I knew from personal experience and from listening to hundreds of others that abortion often left serious emotional wounds. Eva already struggled with so many things, but at least she wouldn't be adding abortion to the list.

"The threat of legal action didn't go unnoticed so my next step was to contact Ohio Right To Life. Within hours I received a call from an attorney offering his pro-bono services. He advised that we have as little involvement as possible with government agencies.

"This was difficult advice to follow since I had to weigh the risks involved with Eva's mental illness. I knew there was a possibility of something going terribly wrong and didn't want to have any doubts regarding my involvement.

"A few weeks later, we checked in for one of her medical appointments and were told by the receptionist that I could *not* go in with her. After an hour she came out of the exam room telling me she'd changed her mind- she wanted to get the abortion after all. Several staff members and the doctor were standing nearby, waiting to see my reaction.

"I told her calmly. 'Okay, I can take you in, like I said I would.' The staff seemed relieved with my answer and went on their way and the doctor handed me the number for the clinic.

"'Now that she's past the 12-week mark, it'll be more complicated,' she told me, her glare implying that I was to blame and that I needed to make things right by making sure she followed through.

"As soon as we were in the car, I asked Eva what they had said that made her change her mind. Her answer was, 'She told me if I gave birth to my baby, that they'd be taken from me and put in foster care, and everything that happened to me would happen to them. Liz, do you think aborted babies go to heaven?'

"I told her I believed they did. Eva's logical response took me by surprise. 'Then I want to get the abortion. I'd rather have my baby go right to heaven, instead of having all those things happen to them. Can I use your phone?' she asked.

"I remained in the car while she made the call. I could hear the woman on the line promising that it'd be painless and no big deal and because she was so far along she wouldn't even be awake. Eva looked at me and asked if she needed to decide right now. I told her she didn't and that she could get one months from now if she wanted."

"Three days later when I picked her up, she handed me a drawing and said she changed her mind again and did not want an abortion. I'd already seen many of her drawings, all of tormented demon-type figures, but this one was of a beautiful dark-haired baby boy.

"The staff at the pregnancy resource center helped us find a doctor who'd care for both Eva *and* her child. We were happy to hear that because she was out of the first trimester, she could now be treated with medication that wouldn't harm the baby. We were also reassured that I could be with her during all the exams."

"Where'd she live?" asked Meg.

"Finding housing turned out to be the biggest challenge. She had three days' worth of hotel vouchers left when we met. There were many group-housing options but we were turned away due her mental condition.

"I started to consider my usual network for housing but, after several middle-of-the-night incidences involving police and men visiting at the hotel, it became apparent she wouldn't be a fit for that either. Her disability income helped but it wasn't enough to cover rent for her own place. My mom allowed her to sleep on her couch while I searched.

"Eva loves my mom, whom everyone calls Nana. Eva told her the reason she had to sleep with her shoes on was because that way she could jump up and run whenever she needed to. It was a huge sign of trust when she started removing them at night.

"During an online search, I located a home for pregnant women about an hour away. While visiting, Eva became angry about not being able to smoke. She ran out of the house and disappeared into the night. After driving around the dark streets calling out her name for nearly an hour, I had no choice but to return home.

"She called three days later, saying 'Living on the streets is fine, but I'm scared for my baby.' After she asked me to come get her, I told her I would but only on the condition that she'd be willing to *consider* adoption for the baby. She agreed and asked for help with the decision."

"Eva spent a few more nights at my mom's house while I continued to search for housing *and* now a couple to adopt the baby. The first two I checked with weren't interested but offered support and encouragement which was invaluable. This is where Karina and her husband enter the story," Liz ended with a gesture and a smile aimed at Karina.

Karina began. "Early in our marriage, we discussed adoption and discovered we were both interested. We were financially stable and it seemed that life on our farm was perfect for raising kids. After our first two came one right after the other, we decided to take a break for a couple of years. When the time was right to have another baby, we didn't get pregnant right away like we had before.

"After several months of trying, we concluded that perhaps now was the time to move forward with an adoption. We started the process to adopt from Ethiopia and had just completed and sent off the legal forms at the end of January when we discovered we were pregnant. The agency put the adoption on hold because it's their policy to wait until the youngest child in the family is at least six months old.

"In early May, I had a little extra time on my hands while in town shopping, so I dropped in to browse at a small thrift shop. I wasn't looking for anything in particular, but I found a pair of baby boy shoes and, while paying, struck up a conversation with the owner. When I was turning to leave, she said, 'You know, you seem like a very nice person with lots of good connections. Let me tell you about this local girl who's decided to give up her baby for adoption.'

"She proceeded to tell me about Eva, who'd come into the store a few days earlier. She asked if she could give me the number of the woman helping her. Perhaps I could help find someone to adopt the baby.

"I agreed, amazingly not even thinking about *us* filling the role. After all, we were pregnant and still on the waitlist for an Ethiopian adoption. However, I figured for sure I could find someone in our community. When I got home, I casually mentioned to Trevor my experience at the thrift store. He immediately urged me to call Liz, asking, 'What if we're the ones who're to adopt this baby?'

"I was shocked. The thought hadn't even crossed my mind but I agreed to call her anyway. After Liz gave me a snapshot of Eva's story and I told her a bit about our family, we set a time to meet at a coffee shop. Liz recounted everything she knew, how they'd met, her medical condition, and the reality of her lifestyle. She was adamant that it'd be a miracle if this child survived.

"As I listened to Trevor and Karina," interjected Liz, "I couldn't believe how perfect it sounded. They were fourth generation dairy farmers living in a small town, surrounded by grandparents, aunts, uncles, and many cousins. Karina had a teaching degree, and because she was home schooling the children and Trevor worked the farm, he was able to be very involved with raising them. I'd read that children born to parents struggling with Eva's mental illness were less likely to develop it if they grew up in a rural setting."

"We told Liz we'd prayed about the whole situation and felt that if God led us in this direction, we'd follow him wherever he took us," Karina continued. "She told us she was ending her search and that she'd be praying this baby would grow up on our farm.

"When we met Eva a week later at the same coffee shop, she had many questions for us. Would we tell her baby about her, what would we tell them, could she ever see them? We explained that we'd be very open with the child regarding their birth mom, that we'd tell them that she'd been very brave and strong when choosing to give them life. We assured her that she could visit them, that she could choose their name, and that we wanted to help her as well.

"We gave Eva a written profile telling all about our family, and she later told Liz she liked us and wanted us to adopt her baby. We were relieved when Liz figured out housing for her. At the end of June, we met with an attorney to begin the the process of an open adoption. It seems amazing that we'd started the adoption process, become pregnant, *and* found out about Jordan's birth mom all within months. Looking back we realized we probably wouldn't have been ready to adopt if we hadn't already begun the process."

"Shortly after meeting Karina & Trevor, I bought a camp trailer and found a friend willing to place it on her property," Liz added in. "Eva made payments towards the trailer and for rent on the property. Everything was stable for a while. Bud the farm dog wasted no time making himself at home in the camper. She loved to visit the horses and sit in the shaded grassy area between the creek and her small home. Because she was close to both my mom's and my homes, caring for her was easy. We came to know the smart, sweet, and extremely lovable parts of her."

"But then the late-night troubles began once again and there were several times when I spent hours comforting her over the phone. She was frightened of the dark, so it wasn't unusual for her to stay up all night. She'd found a new boyfriend and was concerned that he was stalking around the camper and wanted to hurt her. I had to set limits on the number of times she could call at night, and one night she needed more comfort than I was able to give. She ended up calling the police and then my mom."

"The officers were there when mom and I arrived. Eva ran up to us wide eyed and hysterical and was begging us to take her away. Another family living on the property had been disturbed, and it was clear that this seemingly ideal housing arrangement had come to an end. My mom took her home for the remainder of that night, and the camper was towed there the next day.

"The next morning over breakfast, as I shared the previous night's activity with Charles, he expressed his concern about the emotional toll I was experiencing. I was also training heavily for a 40-day fundraiser walk around the state that was scheduled to begin in a few months. Eva was due to deliver around the beginning of November, so I'd also have to find support for her during that time.

"Charles asked me to choose between the two-training for the walk or helping Eva. I told him I couldn't do that-since I believed they were interconnected. My reasoning was that neither the walk, nor the post-abortion study that led to her meeting me, would have happened if it weren't for my abortion. I made that poor choice because of fear, and I was no longer going to let fear rule my life. Yet, I knew neither endeavor would be possible without his support, and the thought of choosing one over the other was unbearable, so I asked him to make the choice for me. He called later that day to tell me he agreed and that he'd support me in both."

Liz continued, "A few days later during another episode of anxiety, Eva called to tell me there were creatures in Nana's house and that Nana had also become one and was trying to kill her. I immediately drove over and asked her to gather her stuff and wait for me in the car. My mother had been generous in housing her several times. It was clear I was now asking too much of her.

"With Eva asleep in the car I drove to the hospital. Sitting in the crowded lobby, I shared everything with the same chaplain who'd helped in the past. I explained what had taken place since our last encounter and attempted, but was unsuccessful, in holding back the tears. I asked him for a few more hotel vouchers.

"Just then I noticed Karina checking in at the reception desk. 'She's the woman wanting to adopt the baby' I told the chaplain. He looked over, commented that she looked very nice and said he was surprised she'd be interested in adopting when she was already pregnant. Then he returned to the matter at hand.

"After asking about Eva's whereabouts, he gently told me that he could see this was taking a great toll on me. He said he couldn't give her any more housing vouchers as she'd already gone over the maximum amount. Clearly I'd done everything I could. Then he gave me a piece of paper with an address on it and recommended I drive her to the homeless shelter in Cleveland. He said he was sorry and went on his way.

"Feeling defeated and devastated, I took the paper and fully intended to follow through with his recommendation."

"I was at the hospital for a routine prenatal test," Karina shared. "I saw Liz talking with the chaplain and went over as soon as he left. She said she'd run out of housing options. She tearfully told me she was all out of options and was going to drive her to the homeless shelter. She didn't know what else to do and had to let her go. I asked her to hold off for one more night and said I'd go home and see if I could find a place for her to stay for the summer.

"Later that day, Trevor and I discussed housing Eva ourselves. I was hesitant since I'd seen the toll it was taking on Liz, but I remember Trevor saying firmly, 'If we are going to save this baby, this is what we need to do.' We called Liz the next day with our answer. We would take her in.

"The next day, we moved her to our home, setting up the camper in our front yard," Karina continued. "The first week was extremely difficult and I had very little hope she'd be able to stay. We were already physically and emotionally drained. She didn't have a single day and night without having a panic attack. She would pace, shake, mutter, and yell in rapid tirades, often for hours. We were needed 'round' the clock to help her through the episodes.

"Amazingly, we made it through the first week. She ended up on our couch most nights, thinking there were people trying to break into her camper and hurt her. She tried to take her life on several occasions, because this would be better than the tortures she was sure to experience at the hands of her unseen foes. One night she ran away, as she believed we were conspiring against her.

"The following month was a blur with the calendar full of doctor appointments and counseling visits all taking place 45 minutes away.

"Now, because of her medication and, I believe, the pregnancy hormones, we began to see her true self- a loving, gracious, and giving person who was full of life. Her talents began to shine. She drew amazing pictures and played the piano beautifully. She loved giving gifts even though she had no money. Things like pictures she drew, items from the food bank, pretty stones she'd found or flowers she'd picked.

"The change we saw in her was such a relief, and we began to see the light at the end of the tunnel. We started preparations for adopting the baby, rather than simply being consumed with getting Eva through another day. She grew to love us and we her. She was full of gratitude for all we did for her and was excited about us adopting her baby. She met many of our friends and family. She would meet random people in our community and tell them that we were adopting her baby.

"In the meantime, we were not telling anyone this, because we knew she could simply vanish the next day and we'd never see her again. Because she lived completely in the moment and acted on every whim, we became convinced that only God could see this adoption through to completion.

"Her low-income housing in town came through right after I gave birth to our third child. We wondered if she'd simply disappear because we lived so far away, and Liz and her mom were away on a mission trip. But, amazingly, she didn't. She loved her new apartment and called almost daily with plans for her future. She wanted to take college classes, get a job, learn how to drive. We expected to get a call any day saying she was in labor. And since she was a heavy smoker, we were prepared to have a small, sickly baby- most likely a preemie- to care for. The fact that she was doing so well on her own was unbelievable."

"Yep, she was calling me nearly every day as well," Liz said. "And I too was afraid she'd take off. But like Karina said, she loved her apartment. She was able to walk to counseling appointments, medical care, and grocery shopping. I walked into town October 15th after being gone for 40 days. I'll never forget the joy I felt seeing Eva at the front of a large group of supporters. From afar I could see her huge smile and her very large belly. So how's that for a long-winded answer to your question about where she lived?" asked Liz with a giggle.

"Amazing, but you can't just stop there! What about his birth?" begged Heather, with Meg nodding in agreement.

"A few weeks later Eva called to let me know she was having contractions," Liz continued. "I kept her on the phone to establish they were happening often enough to warrant a trip to the hospital. My mom and I helped check her in and were waiting for the elevator when she asked the question

I'd been anticipating and had actually rehearsed the answer to.

"'Liz, do you remember how you promised you'd be there for me no matter what I decided?' she asked. 'What if I changed my mind and decided to keep my baby; would you still help me?' I told her I would but then asked her if she wanted to hear what I'd say to the judge if it ended up in court.

"After another contraction she told me she would like to know. I told her I'd have to say that I felt the child would be better off being raised by the Parrishes. She didn't respond and I didn't pursue it since she was facing what I could only imagine would be one of the hardest things any mother could do. Something I wish I'd been brave enough to do."

"I called Karina and Trevor when we learned she was in active labor. They made the trek to the hospital with Stoller, their six-week-old son, and were planning to sleep in the parking lot in a camper on the back of their truck. Fortunately the hospital staff let them use one of the empty patient rooms as their home base.

"Eva was in good spirits, laughing and joking between contractions while she labored on. The sun was just coming up when it was time. When the contractions were too much, she retreated to a time and place far away.

"'Liz, why didn't my mother want me?' She cried out."

"'Oh, honey, I'm sure she wanted you. She just wasn't able to take care of you.' I answered.

"'I wanted my mommy.' she whimpered."

"'I know, dear,' I said, thinking how blessed I was to never have to wonder about my mother's love for me.

"'Liz, will you be my mommy?' she pleaded.

"'Right here, right now: yes Eva. I'll be your mommy,' I promised.

"I remained near her head, stroking it and speaking words of encouragement, while my mom and Karina each supported a leg. The contractions were hard and fast now and Eva's deeply imprinted need for the woman who gave life to her became the main focus as she repeatedly called out my name.

"What an amazing miracle it was to see Jordan's jet black hair appear, then disappear with each contraction. The bright color of his cheeks drew attention to his dimples. When he was fully out Eva cried out, 'my baby, my baby' until they placed him in her arms. What a precious moment to witness as she inspected every beautiful inch of him. Karina, what do you remember about his birth?" Liz asked.

"Both Trevor and I were very excited, but I had a lot of trepidation as well. We didn't talk about it too much, but I doubt that Trevor had as many reservations as I did. Reservations probably isn't the right word, more just fears that she'd change her mind as soon as she saw him. I had no doubt at all that I wanted him as my son. I guess I feared an emotional battle and that we'd all would have to convince her to give him up. I hate confrontation and seeing others hurting, so I feared my own strength wasn't enough to handle it.

"She'd become so special to us by then- like a little sister- that we desperately wanted to make a good decision. However, at the same time I felt a little guilty because that *good decision* that would give us the greatest gift, would bring her immense pain. Trevor had a lot more faith through it all, or maybe he was just able to distance his emotions. I would say excitement was the biggest emotion for both of us, though."

"Yes, I'd say the room was spinning with a full pallet of emotions: joy, fear, pain, and heartache," Liz continued while turning back towards Heather and Meg.

"Jordan was placed in a rolling bassinet and moved into the hallway where Trevor was waiting to meet him. After Trevor returned Jordan to the room, Karina asked Eva if she could nurse him. She agreed, then asked me to call the attorney because she was ready to sign the papers.

"I have a beautiful snapshot in my mind of Trevor and Karina sitting in the window seat with the sun's rays slicing through the room. Trevor held Stoller, while Karina cradled

Jordan to her breast. He wasted no time latching on and receiving continued life from her.

"I felt conflicted between the astounding scene by the window and feeling concern for the young woman in the bed. However, there was consolation in knowing that, because of the sacrifices made by many, the greatest by Eva herself, she'd never have to live with the realization she'd ended his life.

"The attorney came the next day with the papers and was careful to make sure Eva understood what she was agreeing to. After signing, she was anxious to leave for home. A few days later, reflecting back on the experience, Eva told me she believed this had been the greatest thing she'd done in her life."

Meg

The story captivated Meg because she knew firsthand what Eva had avoided by choosing adoption for her child. It *wasn't* easy living with the memory of the choice she made, but it at least seemed possible now.

She'd been learning constructive ways to process the emotions she felt when seeing babies, pregnant woman, and the men by their side. She was no longer burdened by the nightmares, the need to escape, or the shame. She was blown away by the realization of how much had changed in just a few months. Now, instead of wanting to end her life, she was doing well in school, had overcome her drug addiction, and was beginning to feel a stirring to help others.

She knew of at least three girls who had abortions and was reasonably sure there were more. *How were they doing?* she wondered. *Were they having nightmares like she used to? Were they numbing themselves with drugs and alcohol?*

She thought of one girl who committed suicide shortly after her boyfriend broke up with her. The dots were connecting now. Rumor had it she'd had an abortion, and until now Meg never thought it could have been a contributing factor. It didn't turn out to be the easy option the poster in the girl's locker room portrayed it to be.

All the high school girls had seen it.

It was a photo of a happy girl at her high school graduation. The caption read 'Don't let *anything* keep you from your dreams. We offer solutions that are safe, simple, and affordable.' At the bottom was a number for the local health clinic.

Meg would never be able to replace her child, but she might be able to save others. And for those girls who'd already had an abortion, perhaps her story would encourage them to find healing.

"Does Jordan know all this about his birth mom?" Meg asked Karina.

"Yes, just like we promised, we've been open with Jordan all along. They had limited contact during his early years because seeing him was very hard for her. He was about four when he started asking questions. We were looking at his baby book and he saw one of his ultrasound photos. He asked if that was when he was in my tummy so I once again told him about Eva.

"I don't think he really understood until a few months later when we showed him a video we took right after his birth. Eva was holding him, stroking his head and telling him how much she loved him. I asked if he wanted to meet her and he said he did. The timing couldn't have been better because that's about when Eva's treatment changed and her condition really improved. Going forward we made sure he saw her at least once a year, and we called her every week."

"It's so cool you got to nurse him right after birth. Was it hard when you didn't even know if he'd be yours?" asked Heather.

"Yeah, it was pretty hard at first. In fact it felt like I was nursing someone else's baby." Karina admitted. "I really didn't start bonding with him until the adoption became final six weeks after his birth. We had some additional barriers to go through due to his birth father's Native American heritage. Our attorney had to contact the tribe his father belonged to in order to make sure that no one from that tribe wanted to adopt him. Looking back, I was probably protecting my heart. Fortunately, Trevor had more faith than I did and so was able to bond with him right from the start."

"What happened with Eva after the birth?" Meg asked.

"Well, we had her set up with everything she needed, but like many who suffer from her mental conditions, she stopped taking her medicine." Liz continued, "In no time, the hallucinations returned and she began to wander the streets at night. She was picked up by the police, then admitted to the state hospital. She spent a little over a year there and then was placed in a group home where she stayed for about three years. My mom and I visited her nearly every month. Eventually we were allowed to take her shopping with us for several hours at a time.

"She flourished at the group home, with the staff monitoring her visitors, handling her money, and making sure she kept up on her personal hygiene. She was also taught to give herself several shots a day in order to manage some new medical conditions. We were elated when a new medication was discovered that allowed her to live a normal life going forward. Currently she's living out west. She and her husband have twin boys and a brand new baby girl."

"Wow," exclaimed Heather. "Can I get her contact information? I'd love to send her a thank-you note."

"I'd be happy to give it to you, or you could tell her in person next week," suggested Liz. "She would've come sooner but couldn't fly so close to delivery."

"Cool! I can't wait to meet her. Now it all makes sense. Thanks, ladies, for filling us in," exclaimed Heather.

"Yes, thank you!" agreed Meg.

Paul

Later that evening, Paul strolled into Heather's room just in time to hear the final comment at the end of her Spanish lesson, "No puedo esperar para sostener a mi bebé," Heather recited passionately as she sat in bed and completed her lesson.

"Hey, Hon. I have no idea what you just said, but I brought you some really good food," he admitted, setting down several bags.

"Oh, yes! I'll happily use that as an excuse for sitting up again."

Paul opened the steaming boxes, compliments of one of the nearby food carts. "So what's the news on the home front today?" he asked.

"The doctor says we're past the point where they'd stop the labor, but he wants me to continue bed rest as he hopes we'll make it at least one more week."

"Well, I can't imagine news any better that that," he declared, attempting to wrap his arms around Heather.

"And I think I just may have settled on a name for our little girl. What do you think about Eva?" asked Heather.

"I really like it," he replied. "How'd you come up with it?"

The steam from Heather's food dissipated while she shared the events of her day.

Paul's food grew cold as well, his appetite instantly replaced by panic during the all-too-familiar account of a past client he now clearly remembered. *Thank goodness I never burden her with the details of my client's lives*, he thought to himself.

Paul watched Heather's gestures grow passionate while she described the coercive conversation from Liz's perspective. He didn't want her to realize he was the one applying pressure that would have ended Jordan's life. He needed her to believe that his work was helping people. Even more importantly, he needed to believe that himself.

She told him about the Garden of Hope and that she really wanted to memorialize their other children there, but first they'd have to choose names. She asked if he'd help her do that. She also insisted on showing him the video of Liz's speech. He remembered being very frustrated with Liz back then but now understood why she couldn't agree to convince Eva to get an abortion.

She was just one of many he'd counseled towards abortion. He'd been trained to believe it was the best thing for the women but now wasn't so sure. The paradigm shift had him feeling as if he were standing on unstable ground.

If he accepted that Eva getting an abortion might have harmed her, what was he supposed to do with the realization that it might have also harmed some of the others?

Then Paul asked himself how it would have affected him if she *had* gotten it? Most of the time he was grateful for his ability to apply logic. But as the answer came, he only wished he could turn it off. *Jordan would not have been born, Heather would not have been rescued, and rather than visiting her here, he'd be at a gravesite instead.*

Paul was unable to hide the outward signs of the battle raging within.

"Are you not feeling well Paul?" Heather asked with concern.

"No, no, I'm fine, it was just a crazy day at work. I'm doing my best to let it go," he lied.

"I'm just thinking Eva would be an awesome name, kind of like a full-circle tribute. See, if it hadn't been for her bravery in choosing life for Jordan, our little one and I wouldn't be alive. Are you okay with the name, or do you want to think about it?" she asked.

"Eva it is!" Paul agreed, holding up his paper cup for a toast.

Eva

A few days later, a taxi driver thanked Eva for the generous tip as he let her out near the main entrance to the hospital. Their conversation had been enjoyable during the short drive from the airport, and he smiled when he saw her stopping in the lobby, holding up her baby to give her a good view of the fully decorated Christmas tree.

Eva couldn't wait to see Jordan again. *Had it really been seven months since the last time?* she asked herself.

Holding her baby close, she entered the room quietly. She saw a young girl in the corner reading and listening to music on her headphones. Surrounded by textbooks, binders, a box of granola bars, a backpack, and a guitar, she appeared to be settled in for the duration, however long that may be.

Next she saw Karina, sitting near the bed crocheting a purple and pale green baby blanket. The two women hugged, pulled away, then hugged again.

"This is Diana. I named her after Nana," Eva announced with a proud smile. "We're going to visit her this afternoon!"

"She's beautiful, just like you, and I love her name," proclaimed Karina. "I'm almost finished with her baby blanket. Should come in handy as we're expecting more snow later today."

"Well, I've never liked snow myself but Jordan tells me he really does. Has he moved any more than his hands and feet?" she asked while stepping over to his bedside.

"Not yet, but the staff is telling us to watch for it as it could happen any time," replied Karina, her voice filled with hope.

"He looks better than I expected," remarked Eva, a few tears running down her face, right over the forced smile on her lips.

"Well," said Karina with a mischievous grin and a hand motion suggesting Meg join them, "We can thank this young lady for his improvement over the last few weeks. There seems to be a direct connection between the amount of time she spends in the room and the response we see."

Meg

Meg, embarrassed by the compliment, yet loving to hear it, shyly joined Karina and Eva for introductions, then returned to her studies.

Meg *was* spending most of her time with Jordan and wouldn't want it any other way. She was no longer required to attend the therapy sessions, she was nearly finished with the post-abortion healing program, and she continued to excel in her classes.

She'd told her parents about the abortion. They were heartbroken for both her and themselves yet relieved to know she was healing. It would take time before they could fully trust she was done with the drugs, but the changes they'd seen in her were enough to give them hope.

Wendy had told Meg she was thrilled to have her sister and best friend back. It'd been difficult for Meg to face the anger she felt towards Wendy, but after expressing it, the power it held over her seemed not quite so ominous.

Wendy had looked confused when Meg apologized for denying her a niece or nephew. Wendy's many questions were answered, and after the tears subsided, Meg heard the words that would break down the last bit of resentment she felt: "I'm sorry for encouraging you to choose abortion."

Now, there was only one more thing Meg needed in order for her life to be the best she could ever imagine. She wouldn't give up until he woke. Only then could she find out if the incredible feelings she had for him were mutual.

Karina

Tossing and turning that night, Karina realized the couch in the hospital lounge was not nearly as comfortable as the bed at the house *but* was a huge improvement over the chair in Jordan's room. Her light sleep was interrupted by the intrusive sound of her ringing phone.

"Karina, I'm so sorry to call in the middle of the night. This is Chuck, Meg's father. I asked her for your number since she spent so much time at the hospital. I just discovered she's not home, and I can't call her since her phone's here. She's usually home around ten. When did you last see her?"

"She was in Jordan's room when I left about 9:30. I'm still at the hospital; let me go to the room right now. Hold on."

Karina checked the time on her phone as she walked quickly down the empty hallway. It was 3:38 am. *Please let her be there,* she thought.

Karina's fears dissipated instantly. "Meg's here," she whispered into the phone. "Sound asleep in the chair."

"Oh, thank God," he replied. "Don't bother waking her, and thank you so much."

Peeking in once again, Karina's suspicions of their affection for one another were confirmed. Meg had pulled the chair over to Jordan's bedside, and for the first time since the accident, he was lying on his side. She was in a deep sleep with her head resting on the edge of the bed, their right hands intertwined.

Karina's heart swelled with emotion as she focused in closer and saw that the fingers on Jordan's left hand were gently stroking her hair. She could see a slight smile on his lips and his eyes halfway open, gazing affectionately at Meg.

Now feeling like an intruder on a very personal moment, Karina retreated to the lobby and called Trevor to share the good news. She figured he wouldn't be at all concerned about the time of night, and she was right. He'd drive in as soon as he could line up help for the farm.

It was all she could do to resist rushing back into the room. Instead, she visited the nurse's station, updating them on her discovery. The nurse in charge was paged and she soon joined Karina in the lounge.

Thrilled to hear about the progress, the nurse explained that Jordan would most likely be disoriented for several days. She encouraged Karina to continue talking, playing music, and asking him questions. It was also important to explain to him that it was okay if he *could* not or *did* not want to respond, and that it was normal to be very sleepy. He'd most likely be in the hospital for a few more weeks, then moved to a rehabilitation center for physical, speech, and emotional therapy. The nurse also warned her that it could be months before the full extent of his recovery would be known.

Karina knew better than to attempt falling back to sleep, so she grabbed some coffee and settled in with her laptop to do some research on post-coma rehabilitation.

The sun was just peeking above the horizon when Meg stumbled into the lounge area. Her disheveled hair and sleepy eyes did little to distract from the ear-to-ear grin on her face.

Karina took a mental snapshot of the beautiful young lady, and wondered, *could this be my daughter-in- law some day?*

"Jordan's awake," Meg stammered. "He can't talk but he can move and smile." She had so much more to say, but was unable to as the rush of emotions rendered her voice useless.

"I know," Karina replied, standing up and enveloping Meg in her arms. After a moment, she continued. "I looked in the room earlier because your dad called and was worried."

"I didn't mean to fall asleep," Meg replied, pulling away from the embrace and lowering her head. "I was playing the guitar and noticed that rather than tapping to the beat, his fingers were motioning for me to come over. When I did, I put my hand in his and he squeezed it so hard and smiled. I just couldn't leave and must have dozed off. I'm so sorry."

Meg's face showed a tint of red as she frantically tried to straighten the tangled mass of hair perched on top of her head.

"Oh, don't be sorry, you're already dear to me, and now it appears my son feels the same way." Karina continued reassuringly, "I couldn't be happier! Let's go back to the room!"

Trevor and Eva, who'd shared the elevator on their way up, converged with Karina and Meg right outside Jordan's room.

6. TURNING TIDE

Jordan

The fact that Jordan could hear people coming in the room was nothing new, but now he could *see* them as well. His face was slow in communicating the thrill he felt as Meg, Karina, Trevor, and Eva came into focus.

Meg looks good, really good. A change from the times her recently saw her at school, he thought.

Mom and dad look the same. So does Eva, except she's thinner. I wonder if her new baby's a boy or girl. It's so tiny. I want to hold it. I can't wait to see all my family again.

Why can't I talk? Why is the skin on my back so stiff? Why can I only hear out of one ear? I wonder if the lady survived, or was that all a dream? I remember pulling her out of the car. Meg was in the other car.

Before Jordan knew it, he was overcome by drowsiness. He tried shaking his head, but it only helped for a moment. He feared that if he fell asleep again, he wouldn't be able to wake up. After his mom assured him the drowsiness was normal, he stopped fighting and dozed off instantly.

He woke to the sound of a crying baby and was happy to see everyone was still in the room. His thoughts seemed less chaotic now, and it felt as if his brain clicked into overdrive.

Many memories came flooding in and it seemed easier to separate dreams from reality. But as each answer developed, it only brought up several more questions.

"Rumor has it there's good reason to celebrate today!" announced a newcomer as she entered the crowded room.

"Hi Jordan. I'm Jorie, one of the hospital counselors. It's such a joy to officially meet you. I've got a tool here that should help you communicate."

Jordan couldn't remember this voice but didn't care. She had something he really wanted to get his hands on.

"We'll be starting voice therapy in a day or so. Let's give this a try in the meantime," she explained while handing the iPad to Jordan.

The program on the home screen offered many options. There were icons of food, water, a person sleeping or taking a bath. He had choices of simple phrases, such as "I'm tired" or "Please turn off the light" and there was also the option to type what he wanted to say. His hand motions were still jerky, so he started with the simple icons.

His first choice was easy. Jordan made a shaky sweeping motion with one arm, his pointer finger extended letting everyone in the room know the message was for them. He then pushed the heart icon and the words "I love you" could be heard in the unemotional robotic voice. His next words were "thank you." Then, reluctantly, he chose the icon of the person sleeping. "I'm tired."

Trevor suggested the group moved to the lounge area, and as they were doing so, the robotic voice could be heard once again.

"Meg stay? Song?"

Meg

More than happy to oblige Jordan's request, Meg pulled the chair near the bed, picked up the guitar, and started strumming. With the iPad turned so she couldn't see the screen, Jordan labored on his next message. There wasn't an icon for what he needed to ask, but that wasn't going to stop him.

His erratic reflexes hindered progress and Meg could sense his growing frustration as he repeatedly cleared the screen.

"It's okay, Jordan; you're tired. How about we talk after you rest?" she suggested.

Jordan's expression made it clear that whatever he needed to say was not only important in content, but in timing as well. He pulled up the previous comment and pushed "repeat. "

"Meg stay? Song?" the robotic voice asked again while Jordan did his best to provide a pleading facial expression.

"Okay, I won't go anywhere," she reassured him.

Jordan, relieved, returned to his mission and spent several minutes battling both his physical limitations and mounting fatigue. Finally, with questioning eyes, he turned the iPad towards Meg and pushed the speaker button.

"When I'm better, will you go out with me?" the robotic voice inquired.

Their eyes met with a connection deeper than either had ever experienced. It was as if he were seeking a reflection of his future deep within her eyes. Meg didn't turn away, and her slight nod along with an ever-so-delicate smile let Jordan know he'd found it.

Sleep came quickly for Jordan while Meg once again gave voice to the words and melody that'd recently erupted from her wounded soul.

Didn't know Him well in my younger days,
It showed in my thoughts and it showed in my ways.
Returning a gift that was sent from above
not knowing then it was something I'd love.
Becoming aware of what my choice really meant.
The pain and the sorrow, too much to repent.
So I buried my anguish, it was best that I hide,
and deep in the night, I just lay there and cried.

I don't know love, I don't know joy,
I don't know peace.
There's none inside of me. There's none inside of me.

And there's no patience and goodness or kindness

for anyone to see, for anyone to see.

Gentleness passed by me and faithful I can't be.

Self-control can't find me,

so lonely I will be, so lonely I will be.

Much later, a sister, she reached out to me

There's others who've suffered, come join us, you'll see.

We'll show you a path that will lead you back home,

It's not easy to follow, but you won't be alone.

I've learned that I'm loved even thought I can't pay.

I've learned I'm forgiven, so to Him I will say:

You gave me love, you gave me joy, you gave me peace,

beyond my wildest dreams, beyond my wildest dreams.

And now there's patience and goodness and kindness

That overflow from me, that overflow from me.

Gentleness has found me and faithful I can be,

Self-control will bind me, for you have set me free,

Yes, you have set me free.

Through Him I have joy and a reason to live,

There's so much I can offer, so much I can give.

Seeing through the pretending, the things that we do-

The pain in your soul, my heart aches for you.

He's strong and yet gentle and He forgives us each day.

He wants me to share... so to you I'll now say:

He'll give you love, He'll give you joy, He'll give you peace

beyond your wildest dreams.

And you'll have patience and goodness and kindness

that overflow it seems, that overflow it seems.

Gentleness will find you, and faithful you will be.

Self-control will bind you,

For He will set you free, yes, He will set you free.

7. NEW LIFE

Heather

The moment Heather woke, she knew it was going to be a memorable day. Her body felt different, and her voracious appetite was overshadowed only by her strong sense of anticipation.

She always looked forward to her late morning visit with Karina, and today would get to meet Eva as well.

Waddling down the hall, Heather was taken aback by the 'Do Not Disturb' sign on Jordan's door, her first thought being that something had gone terribly wrong.

A nurse passing by noticed her concerned look. "He's just resting. The family all moved to the lounge," she said with a smile.

Judging by the looks on everyone's face in the lounge, she reasoned there must be some *really* good news, and she didn't have to wait long to hear it.

"Jordan woke up," Karina shouted as she ran over and gave Heather an awkward sideways hug.

"That's wonderful! Is he responding?"

"He can understand us but as of yet is unable to talk. He's using an iPad to communicate."

"I can't wait to meet him!" Heather exclaimed, resting both hands on her belly. As she did so, the expression on her face transitioned from joy to concern. "I'm having contractions, she whispered. "I need to get back to my room."

"I'm coming with you," Karina reassured her.

Paul

Paul's day at work bore no difference from all the others until a text appeared on his phone. He was halfway through a Power Point presentation he was giving to the staff. He had hoped to sneak a peek without missing a beat in the program, but quickly realized it was futile. His heart leapt as he read the text.

Contractions started, hard to predict how long. Please come ASAP.

On my way, he replied, his audience staring at him in concern.

"Carry on without me. I'll be gone a few days. My little girl's gonna need some cuddles!" he said with a huge smile.

Paul's colleagues stood up and clapped as he packed his gear, happy for this friend who'd left in a hurry many times before only to return devastated.

Though he'd made the trip from work to the hospital many times, never before did it feel like this one. His usually successful measures for squelching the feelings of hope arising within him failed miserably and by the time he arrived, he was filled to the brim.

"Thank you, Karina," he exclaimed, relieved to see his wife was not alone when he rushed in the room.

"My pleasure, you know where to find us if you need anything," she replied, heading out the door.

Paul was excited to show Heather the items he'd put together for their labor kit.

She watched with anticipation as he used the time between contractions to present each one to her. There was the treasured framed photo of the two of them standing near the cliff in Mexico, lemon drops, chapstick, lavender oil, and chewing gum. He saved the best for last.

An old bar napkin he'd discovered taped to the back of the framed photo had been professionally mounted for the occasion. The illustration upon it was a creation from the night the photo was taken. She and Paul, feeling giddy after enjoying a few margaritas, had each contributed to a stick figure family; a mom, a dad, two children, and a dog.

Heather had completely forgotten about the drawing and was thrilled with her husband's thoughtfulness. Together, and only for a moment, they relished the memory of that silly experience long ago. The next contraction, much stronger than all the others, brought them quickly back to the present. She was as ready as anyone could be.

The contraction was just subsiding when Dr. Brauer entered. Moments later after glancing at the monitor and reading the nurse's notes, he stated, "You're 4 cm dilated, it's time to head to the birthing room."

Walking alongside the wheelchair Paul noticed a woman entering the room he knew was Jordan's. It had been 18 years since he'd seen Eva. He'd heard the baby was adopted, that things had gone well for a few months, and then she'd backslid and been admitted to the state hospital. She looked wonderful now, with a baby in her arms. He was happy for her and grateful he'd been wrong, yet he turned his gaze away as they passed. It felt wrong that he couldn't face his daughter's namesake just before she was born.

The next four hours were surreal, and it was a challenge to remain present as Heather's contractions grew in intensity and the space between them grew shorter. Despite Dr. Brauer's reassurance that everything was progressing normally, Paul couldn't seem to quiet the nagging voice taking up residence in his mind. *Everything could change in an instant. What makes you think this one is so different than all the others? Do you really think you deserve to be a father?*

Paul knew he needed help, but where could he turn at a moment like this? Just then he was reminded of his desperate plea in the elevator.

"Heather, I'm sorry, but I need to leave for a short time. Trust me, it's very important and I promise to explain later," he beseeched.

"Make it fast," she pleaded.

Karina was talking with Meg in the lobby and, after a quick exchange with Paul, agreed to take his place at Heather's side. She gave him directions to where he was headed and said a quick prayer for him as they hurried down the hall in opposite directions.

It was easy to find his destination and, as he opened the only door in the hospital adorned with a stained glass window, he felt a great rush of emotions.

Shortly after Paul fell to his knees at the foot of the cross, he was joined by the only other person in the chapel, a farmer giving praise for the life of his son.

"Would you like to talk?" asked Trevor.

"More than you can imagine."

The transaction that took place in the chapel had a profound effect on Paul. The pressing fear and feelings of condemnation over his stance on when life began and the harm he may have caused others had been replaced with things he currently had little understanding of. However, Trevor had assured him that it would come with time. Right now, he needed to be back with Heather.

The two women let out a sigh of relief as Paul rushed into the birthing room. Heather's anger and confusion over his departure had subsided when Karina assured her it was a good thing, and that he'd be a better husband and father as a result.

There was no time for explanations. The smile Paul received from Heather was all he needed. He was ready now.

Jordan

When Jordan awoke the next day, he found himself alone but could still hear Meg's music. He smiled broadly with the realization that she' recorded it for him and the memory that she'd agreed to go out with him.

I'm gonna put everything I have into rehab and make the best of it, no matter how it turns out, he promised himself just before his parents entered the room.

It wasn't long after his parents walked in that he could sense their mixed emotions. They were thrilled he was awake, yet it was difficult to be the bearer of some of the news. Wrestling was out of the question, not only for the season but indefinitely, and with that went the full-ride scholarship offers. He had a tough road ahead of physical rehab, speech therapy, and emotional healing. *But our family knows how to deal with setbacks, he reminded himself.*

Good things had already come out of the accident. He'd saved the lives of two people and, with the exception of losing hearing in one ear, he'd likely make a full recovery. Both his home community and his school had joined forces and held several fundraisers. So far, his state school tuition was 50% funded, and, because of his grades, he qualified for the honors program.

Jordan followed suit when his parents bowed their heads in prayer. Moments later, Meg stepped in the doorway, saw their heads bowed and quickly did the same.

As they finished, Jordan nodded toward the door with a smile. His parents, realizing that Meg had been praying as well, smiled and motioned her in to join them.

"Heather's baby was born healthy!" she announced while moving towards Jordan and his parents.

"Name?" asked Jordan's robotic voice.

Meg smiled mischievously, "Heather wants to tell you herself. Maybe tomorrow, if you feel up to meeting her."

"Okay," he typed, while sticking out his lower lip in a pout.

Meg

Meg cringed when Eva walked in the room a short time later. Up until now, she'd been able to avoid being around babies.

"Diana and I came to say goodbye. She wants to know if you can hold her," Eva she said to her firstborn.

Meg noticed the bright sun, breaking through the clouds and shining in the room, highlighted Jordan's dimples as he adjusted the pillows under his arms and patted them to show he was more than willing to oblige. She felt a lump forming in her throat as she witnessed the young man who tried to save her baby, gently cradling this one. But instead of withdrawing, and seeking a way to numb her feelings, she faced them head on, remembering what she'd learned in her healing program.

She gently reminded herself that she was still grieving her loss, and that it would take time. She no longer had to feel ashamed. Yes, she'd made a poor choice, and the ramifications of that choice had lifelong consequences, but she could choose to no longer be shackled by the shame. She could choose to feel regret instead, and *that* she could live with.

Jordan, with one arm holding Diana, used the other arm to make a comment. He pointed first to his eye, next to his heart, and then lastly to his sister. Then, after repeating the motions, he pointed to Eva.

"I love you, too," Eva replied. "We're heading to the airport now. I'm glad you're doing so well and can't wait 'til you come see us this summer. Diana will be crawling by then, and your brothers are going to want to play checkers with you 24/7!"

Jordan nodded and smiled at the thought.

As Eva said her goodbyes, Jordan kissed Diana's forehead and offered her to Meg, his eyes full of encouragement. *I can do this,* Meg told herself. As she held the baby close to her chest, she tried not to be drawn in to her piercing gaze, but it was no use. Diana babbled and blew bubbles and her fingers tightened around Meg's finger.

She realized how much she wanted one of her own, but knew that it could never replace the one she'd lost. She wouldn't place that unattainable expectation on any future children.

"She's beautiful," Meg declared, carefully handing the baby back to her mom.

"Thank you," Eva replied sincerely, "you are too."

Meg blushed at the compliment and, though it didn't feel natural, allowed herself to believe it.

Eva

"Can we stop and see Heather on your way out?" asked Karina. "She really wants to meet you."

"Of course. Better get going now though," answered Eva as she blew one last kiss to Jordan.

"Eva, I'm very happy to meet you," Heather said after their brief introduction. "Karina's shared so much about you and I just want to say that my my husband and I want to thank you for being so brave."

"You're welcome. I had a lot of help. What's your baby's name?"

"We named her after you. Her name's Eva," replied Heather with a grin.

"Wow, thank you," she whispered bashfully.

"Where's Paul?" asked Karina.

"He just went to get some food. I'm so hungry and, as I'm sure you can relate, the hospital food's gotten old."

"Yes, I *can* relate. Please tell him I'm sorry he didn't get to meet Eva. She's got a plane to catch," apologized Karina as they said their goodbyes.

Traffic was light on the way to the airport and Eva was relieved when Diana fell asleep shortly after takeoff. She needed some time alone with her thoughts.

She couldn't believe a child had been named after her. As she closed her eyes, she went back in time to when she was pregnant with Jordan. She'd expected Liz to give up on her, like so many others had. One of the many times she'd thanked her, she remembered Liz saying she was just *helping her do what she already wanted to do.*

It wasn't easy, but she *had* been brave.

Karina

Sitting in Jordan's room that evening, Karina started the next baby blanket, this one for baby Eva. She was encouraged to see her son starting round three of his physical therapy exercises for the day.

"Jordan, Heather wants to meet you now. Sound okay?" she asked after reading a new text message. An energetic head nod accompanied Jordan's thumbs-up.

He was just finishing his exercises when Heather walked in the room. "It's so nice to finally meet you, Jordan," she said moments later with her hand outstretched. Jordan pressed the 'Thank You' icon and Karina noticed his mouth moving in unison with the robotic voice before he slowly extended his hand for the greeting.

"Baby's name?" he typed.

"It's Eva, named after your birth mom."

"Coo.......!" he exclaimed on his own. Embarrassed by his garbled odd-sounding voice and mispronounced word, he blushed while typing out what he really wanted to say. "Cool," stated the robotic voice.

Karina was thrilled. The first word she'd heard from her son in months had sounded perfect to her.

"My husband and I can't thank you enough for all you've done. We know you've sacrificed a lot because of it, so we plan to make up the difference in your college fund. We know it's not the same as the plans you had, but we're hoping it'll help."

"Dank ooh!" Jordan blurted out. He finished his comment with the iPad and Karina wondered if it was out of habit or due to a possible lump in his throat. "Thank you so much," the robotic voice stated.

Karina knew her son would make good use of his time at school and was grateful for her new friend's generosity.

The next day, as she lay in bed, Karina realized that Jordan's first two weeks awake had passed in a blur. Her son was facing his challenges head-on, as was his custom.

His rate of progress far outpaced the timeline set forth by the specialists, and so plans to move him to the rehab center wing were moved up to the following week.

"He's doing fantastic with his therapy," the speech pathologist had told her. "We won't be needed much longer."

After his time in the rehab center wing, he'd be returning to live with Liz and Charles for the remainder of the school year. He'd be making up his lost credits at school by writing essays about his experience, which would allow him to graduate with his class.

When Karina returned to Jordan's room she noticed him once again practicing his voice lessons. Meg, who was out grabbing lunch, continued to be with him at every possible moment, and Karina was beginning to wonder if it might be time to head home to the farm, perhaps returning only on the weekends.

Paul

Later that day, Paul left work early. He could hardly contain himself as he stopped by the house to open the shades, straighten the kitchen, and place a bouquet of fresh flowers on the dining-room table.

He opened the door to Eva's room, and was overcome by joy at the realization that their home was never going to be the same. Though it'd been nearly three months with Heather in the hospital, the last few weeks had seemed like the longest.

He arrived at the hospital ahead of schedule. Entering the room, he saw all the belongings were packed and ready to go, but where were Heather and Eva?

Inquiring at the nurses' station, he was told they could be found in Jordan's room. He was hoping to avoid going in there- it was easier to send money than to face the young man whose life had once seemed so insignificant to him. He headed down the hall, grateful that it was going to take several trips to get all this stuff to the car.

"Hey, Paul," Heather shouted from Jordan's room as he passed by. "We're in here."

He had no choice but to go in and was relieved to see there was no one there who knew of his past connection. *It would all be coming out soon enough, just not now,* he thought.

Paul saw a young man in the bed, holding Eva, touching her cheeks and searching for her tiny toes under the blanket. Meg, looking nothing like when he first saw her outside the ER, was strumming the guitar in the corner, smiling at Jordan.

Heather introduced the two men, and Paul noticed Jordans' weak handshake was not representative of the confident look in his eyes. He realized it was because of this confidence that he was bringing his family home today. He was flooded with gratitude that his professional training had failed with the case of this man's mother. All he could muster was, "Thank you."

"Hey, Liz, welcome to the party!" Heather exclaimed. "This is my husband Paul, and our daughter Eva. We're on our way home!"

Paul could hardly breathe as he turned around to face Liz, just entering the room. It had been 18 years, but she didn't look much different. He was relieved that although there was recognition on her face, she chose to act as if they were meeting for the first time.

"It's very nice to meet you, Paul. I've so loved getting to know your wife," Liz said calmly, reaching out to shake his hand.

"Thank you, and thank you for helping Eva when she needed it. We've named our little girl after her."

"Well, the truth is, the Parrishes did most of it, but for my part, it truly was a blessing to help her. Her story has the power to change the way people look at the issue," Liz replied with an inquiring gaze.

"Yes, it does," agreed Paul with a nod, before he shifted his gaze longingly towards his daughter, who was still in Jordan's arms.

Jordan carefully offered Eva to Paul, then motioned that he'd like to say something.

Holding his little girl close, Paul waited patiently as Jordan cleared his throat, took a deep breath, and started in. Slowly, and with long pauses between them, came the first four words, "I...bet...you...would...", followed by the rest in perfect speed and cadence, "like to take her home."

"Yes, I would," replied Paul.

And so he did.

A letter from the author

Dear reader,

First of all, thank you for taking this journey with me. My hope is that you've been impacted in a positive way.

If the words in this book brought up some issues you need to talk about with someone, please do not hesitate to reach out. Know that many people struggle with the issues addressed in this book and there is no shame in seeking assistance with the multi faceted emotions which can surface.

There are several resources listed on the next page, and many more can be found online.

I welcome private messages on my Cindy Brunk-Speaker/Writer/Author Facebook page.

Blessings to you.

Cindy

Pregnant ?

Stand up Girl - an online community of women who've been there.

http://www.standupgirl.com/

Care Net - a list of pregnancy resource centers

http://www.care-net.org/find-a-pregnancy-center

Hurting after an an abortion

Silent No More – encouragement and resources

http://www.silentnomoreawareness.org/

Her Choice to Heal – finding spirtual and emotional peace after an abortion.

http://www.amazon.com/Her-Choice-Heal-Spiritual-Emotional/dp/1434768724

Rachel's Vinyard – retreats for healing

http://www.rachelsvineyard.org/

Men

Reclaiming Fatherhood – men dealing with abortion

http://www.menandabortion.info/

Abortion worker

And Then There Were None – helping abortion workers leave the industry.

http://abortionworker.com/

ABOUT THE AUTHOR

Cindy Brunk is an inspiring speaker, writer, and activist whose journey of healing from the aftermath of abortion inspires the hurting and educates those serving in pro-life ministry.

The inspiration for *Love Will* came from personal experience and those shared by others.

In 2010 she walked 683 miles around the state of Oregon visiting 11 memorial gardens for children lost to abortion. The 40-day *Please Say my Name Tour* raised awareness about post-abortion trauma as well as funds for several pregnancy resource centers.

When she's not serving in the ministry, Cindy can be found playing outdoors or spending time with her husband and four adult children.

Made in the USA
San Bernardino, CA
18 April 2016